Damn, but t
thought.

He'd been mesmerised by the sheen of moonlight on her cheeks, the wild profusion of vibrant hair. Had felt his body drawn towards hers. One more second of moonlit madness and he'd have been kissing her.

Kissing Riley Dennison?

The aggravating woman who had caused him more problems than a dozen wives and wreaked more havoc in his house than an earthquake?

The no-sex thing must have him tied in knots. Or something she'd put in his dinner had affected him.

A single bark from one of the dogs made him turn, in time to see Ms Dennison bounding down the grassy slope towards the beach.

And something in the freedom of her movements, the sheer joy with which she ran, made him want to follow.

As a person who lists her hobbies as 'reading, reading and reading', it was hardly surprising **Meredith Webber** fell into writing when she needed a job she could do at home. Not that anyone in the family considers it a 'real' job! She is fortunate enough to live on the Gold Coast in Queensland, Australia, as this gives her the opportunity to catch up with many other people with the same 'unreal' job when they visit the popular tourist area.

Recent titles by the same author:

FOUND: ONE HUSBAND
CLAIMED: ONE WIFE
HEART'S COMMAND
BAUBLES, BELLS AND BOOTEES

REDEEMING
DR HAMMOND

BY
MEREDITH WEBBER

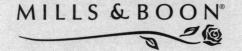

First published in Great Britain 2001
Harlequin Mills & Boon Limited,
Eton House, 18-24 Paradise Road, Richmond, Surrey TW9 1SR

© Meredith Webber 2001

ISBN 0 263 82673 2

Set in Times Roman 10½ on 11½ pt.
03-0701-50430

Printed and bound in Spain
by Litografia Rosés, S.A., Barcelona

CHAPTER ONE

MITCH pulled a pillow over his head to blot out the ringing noise, and tried desperately to recapture his dream. But the peaceful green fields in which he'd been picnicking had vanished, along with the woman who'd looked suspiciously like Celeste but had been far more agreeable.

The ringing wasn't entirely blotted out by the pillow.

And the dream had been replaced by an insistent throbbing behind his eyeballs.

He was in pain!

He sat up and peered at the screen on the clock radio.

Six o'clock.

Surely Mrs Rush was up by six! Why hadn't she answered the door?

The ringing continued.

He stumbled out of bed, cursing his decision to attend Peter Sutton's official-though-a-fortnight-early farewell party the previous evening, and his own weakness in allowing Peter's fiancée to ply him with champagne.

Never had been able to drink champagne!

Staggering down the hall towards the door, desperate to stop the noise which was clanging like out-of-whack cymbals in his head, he ran into Mrs Rush, a voluminous purple robe covering her red and blue striped flannelette pyjamas.

'Why didn't you answer it?' he growled at her, as the garish colour combinations made his already suffering eyes ache even more.

'It's still dark,' she told him, cowering timorously against the wall. 'Anyone could be out there. You hear stories about elderly women being attacked all the time.'

5

'Heaven save me from all women—even ones in dreams!' he muttered to himself as he strode the extra ten paces to the door.

He unlocked the deadbolt, then realised he had another two locks to go. Mrs Rush's precautions against unwanted intruders!

'All right, we're coming,' he yelled through the panels. 'Get your finger off the damn bell.'

The ringing continued, fostering a murderous rage in Mitch's beleaguered body and causing untold agony in his paining, pounding head. He flung open the door and stared at the tall, shadowed figure standing well back on his doorstep.

Not ringing the bell, although the sound persisted.

'Your bell's stuck,' the stranger said. 'I'll take a look at it later if you like.'

Ignoring this offer, which wouldn't have made much sense on the best of days, and driven to desperation by the noise, Mitch turned to the bell apparatus and jabbed the button viciously. Then he hit the control box with the palm of his hand, jabbed again and finally tried to reef the whole thing off the wall.

The reverberations from the ringing continued to hammer in his skull.

'It's an electric bell. It will be connected to power somewhere,' the stranger announced. 'Turning it off at a switch might be easier than murdering it.'

The noise ceased, and Mitch realised Mrs Rush, hovering in the shadows behind him, must have reached the same conclusion. A solution which made him feel more, not less, angry.

'Who the devil are you?' he demanded, turning his attention back to the stranger, whom he could now see more clearly in the strengthening light of dawn.

'Riley Dennison,' she—for it was a she, although a tall one—announced.

'Riley Dennison?'

Mitch repeated the name. It had to be the remnants of champagne in his bloodstream confusing him. He would have shaken his head to clear it, but guessed it would hurt too much.

Tried speech instead.

'The Riley Dennison I knew was shorter than you, definitely larger around the waist and had a deep voice. *My* Riley Dennison was a man!'

The stranger, who for all she was clad in faded blue overalls and had a dark blue cowboy scarf covering whatever hair she might have, was definitely a woman.

She favoured him with a smile which, he guessed, hid a secret glee at his obvious confusion.

'If you're that possessive about your tradespeople, then I'm glad I'm *not* your Riley,' she said. 'He's my dad, but he's hurt his back so I'll be supervising the job.'

She glanced at her watch.

'And we really shouldn't be standing here nattering. The gang's due at seven and I want to check you've cleared the rooms before they start putting up the scaffolding, ready to take off the roof.'

'Take off the roof?' Mitch muttered weakly. He would never drink champagne again! 'You can't take off the roof.'

'Of course we're taking off the roof,' the new Riley announced, and this time she wasn't hiding her glee. 'You can't build an extension—particularly not an upper-level extension—without taking off at least part of the roof. You saw the plans. And Dad explained it all to you.'

'But today? It's Saturday.'

If he added 'and I've got a headache', would she understand?

'Builders work Saturdays, even if doctors don't,' she told

him, and he realised she was as hard and cold as the tools
she probably used. Not the understanding type at all.

'Dr Hammond works all the time,' Mrs Rush put in,
edging closer to come to his defence.

Or to check out the woman!

'Sure!' Riley Dennison said, and Mitch felt his insides
cringe at the derision in her voice.

Could she tell he had a hangover?

See veins throbbing in his temples, blood dripping from
his eyes?

Was that why she was so antsy?

'They're even too busy to check messages on their answering machines,' she added.

'You left a message? To say you'd be here before dawn
this morning?'

Behind him, Mitch heard Mrs Rush scurrying away. As
well she might! He'd grant her the right to not answer the
door in darkness, but to be frightened of an answering machine? Hadn't they had this out before?

Three long strides took him to the phone, where the
flashing red light told him he had messages.

He pressed the rewind and then the play button, and
heard the real Riley Dennison's voice.

'Looks like rain coming up next week, Doc, so I've re-
adjusted my schedule and we'll get started on your roof
tomorrow morning, preparatory stuff. I've done my back
but my deputy will be on site to supervise the boys. Catch
you later.'

The woman didn't say 'I told you so', but she'd moved
into the entry, into the light, and he could read the message
in her eyes. Strange eyes, a blue-green-grey that defied a
colour definition, but danced with delight. At his expense.

'Where will you start?' he asked, hoping he sounded
more practical than he felt. 'Your father, when we talked,

said he won't have to take off the whole roof, just part of it.'

The new Riley pulled a rolled plan from a back pocket. Talk about a fraud! Here supervising the real tradespeople for her dad and trying to look professional!

She spread it on the hall table and jabbed her finger at the front entrance.

He moved closer, although he'd have preferred to retreat, some instinct telling him this woman was out to ruin his day.

'We're here, and the stairs will go up there, taking out that small bedroom. The main bedroom and its bathroom will be left intact, but I think my father suggested you shift the little girl out of her bedroom because there'll be saw-dust and wood shavings flying through the air.'

'She can go into my bedroom when I go,' Mrs Rush, who'd crept back within hearing distance, put in, but Mitch was too fazed by the disruption to follow such a cryptic comment.

'Well, there's nothing much in the spare bedroom,' he told Riley. 'And anyway, if you're only doing preparatory work, nothing need be shifted at this stage. Mrs Rush can do it later.'

Blue-green-grey eyes rolled expressively.

'No one can go into that bedroom while we're working above it,' their owner said, pacing the words so even a slow learner, which she obviously thought him, could under-stand. 'In fact, it will be locked and I'll have the key. If someone drops a claw hammer, it could go straight through the plaster ceiling, and would be likely to kill, or severely maim, whoever is underneath. I thought doctors were sup-posed to be smart.'

They were also supposed to preserve lives, not have mur-derous urges to brain people with claw hammers!

He quelled the urge with difficulty and repeated lamely, 'Well, there's nothing much in that room.'

'Let's have a look, shall we?' Riley Dennison suggested, and, without waiting for his reply, headed down the hall towards the small bedroom.

Which was when Mitch realised exactly what *was* in the small bedroom.

And Olivia, no doubt woken by the noise, came to investigate what was happening in her house.

'Good grief! What is it? A shrine to the Sex Goddess?' Riley Dennison demanded, waving her hand towards the interior of the room.

Mitch heard the phrase he tried to ignore when he saw it printed in papers, and did another inner cringe. Then he peered through the door into the room he never entered and realised it did, indeed, look like a shrine.

'Mrs Rush?' he bellowed. Olivia, startled by his roar, began to cry, and he lifted her into his arms, but Mrs Rush took longer to reappear.

'Well, it's all got to go. If you need it for some perverse reason, then set it up somewhere else,' the ersatz builder said, bowling into the room and gesturing towards ball-gowns hung on padded hangers from the picture rail and diaphanous gowns spread across the single bed.

'You're not allowed to go in there!' Olivia told the intruder, at the same time as Mitch protested he had no need of any of it and, in fact, couldn't imagine why it hadn't been given away years earlier.

'So you knew she wouldn't come back?' Riley said, turning from the display to look directly at him.

Mitch held Olivia more tightly though she was struggling to be put down. No doubt to enter the forbidden room.

'I don't think that's any of your business!' he said frostily. 'You're here to take off the roof.'

'Just as soon as I've cleared this room,' she replied with abundant cheer, frost having no apparent effect on her.

She turned to Olivia.

'You might like some of these things to play dressing-up,' she suggested, and Olivia kicked Mitch in the groin to show she meant business and squiggled to the floor.

'Were these my mummy's dresses?' she asked, the awe in her voice so apparent Mitch felt his heart ache for her.

'I guess they must have been,' Riley replied, squatting down so she was on a level with the four-year old. 'Aren't they pretty?'

Olivia nodded, and reached out tentative fingers to stroke the rich, red, shimmery material of the closest dress.

Wide-eyed, she spun to face her father.

'May I play dressing-up in some of them?'

She looked so sweet and innocent, blue eyes alight with precious hope, unbrushed golden curls rioting around her head. But he had not the slightest doubt that if he said no she'd immediately go into tantrum mode and they'd all suffer—all day!

'I guess you can choose a couple to keep for dressing-up and we'll put the rest away.'

He saw the guileless eyes harden and regretted his choice of words, but before he could amend 'couple' to 'maybe three or four', Riley Dennison had taken over.

'We could pack the rest in special stuff to keep the moths away, then when you're older and going out to parties and balls, maybe some of them will look really beautiful on you. So you can dress up with some now, and keep the others for when you're grown up.'

. For some reason, Olivia, who up to now had shown no understanding of the concept of compromise, seemed to accept this statement.

'What special stuff?' she asked Riley.

'Mothballs. How about you go and find Mrs Rush and

ask her if she has any? And we'll need suitcases, or boxes.
Maybe the special plastic packs for packing clothes in.
Airtight ones. If you don't have any in the house, Mrs Rush
will know where to buy them.'

Olivia skipped away, and Mitch, torn between astonishment at his daughter's behaviour and jealousy that this
woman could produce it, glared at his 'builder'.

'You're here to take off the roof,' he reminded her.

'As if you'd let me forget,' the woman countered. 'But
I want this room cleared before the men get up there. Let's
shift this stuff. We'll be clearing the little girl's room as
well, but we shouldn't interfere with Mrs Rush's privacy,
so what if we dump all this in the main bedroom for the
moment and let Mrs Rush handle the packing later?'

Without waiting for a reply, she scooped the clothes off
the bed and headed unerringly towards his bedroom.

Where she tripped over his trousers, which lay discarded
just inside the door.

'In a hurry to hit the cot last night?' she mused as her
gaze swept along the trail of discarded clothing. 'I hope
there isn't some poor woman cowering in the bathroom,
waiting for the commotion to cease so she can escape.'

Mitch opened his mouth to deny a woman's presence,
but as he also wanted to tell the intruder it was none of her
business who was in his bathroom, and explain it was tiredness which had made him strip off so hurriedly, the words
jammed in his throat and he said nothing.

She flung the armful of clothes on his bed—the last place
he wanted reminders of Celeste—then moved aside to let
him put down what he'd carried.

Only he hadn't carried any, too bemused to do anything
but follow her to see what she'd do next.

'You're supposed to be helping,' she reminded him. 'In
fact, you should be doing it. Dad certainly didn't calculate

time for clearing the rooms. Where are you going to put your daughter's bed? Over here by the window?'

'She can't sleep in here with me!' Mitch protested.

'Spoil your nocturnal activities, will she?' the wretched woman taunted.

'No! I'll disturb her sleep. Getting up and down in the night. Calls coming in. The phone ringing.'

'You can turn down the volume on your phone, and surely get up quietly. Wouldn't you have taken care not to disturb the Sex Goddess when you were called out at night?'

'Will you stop referring to my wife—my ex-wife—that way?'

Riley shrugged.

'It's what the papers call her.'

'I don't give a damn what the papers call her. If I hear you've used that phrase in front of the child—'

'The child? Hasn't she got a name? Olivia, isn't it? Can't you call her that?'

Mitch's hands clenched. Was the penalty for murder less if you could prove it was justified? Right now, a nice quiet police cell was vastly appealing. And by the time he was released on bail—did you get bail for murder? Anyway, by then his hangover might have passed. Not to mention that by the time he came out of jail, proficient at making number plates, Olivia might be married to a rich solicitor willing to indulge her every whim.

That's if her father being a murderer, added to the ferocity of her temper, which would give any sane man pause, didn't spoil her chances at matrimony.

'Don't bother helping. Another dozen trips and I'll have done the lot myself!'

Riley Dennison must have left without waiting for an answer to whatever had prompted his murderous thoughts and had now returned with another armful of clothes to dump on his bed. Any chance of crawling back into it until the drum stopped beating in his head was gone.

So much for his weekend off duty!

With his head pounding and his mouth feeling as if he'd been swallowing sawdust, he followed the woman who was causing all his misery, and watched as she reefed less exotic clothes from hangers in the small wardrobe.

'Here, you carry these,' she ordered, and when Olivia returned to say Mrs Rush would buy some special bags later in the morning, Riley organised her into carrying shoes.

Shoes? Mitch clasped the bundle of clothes to his chest and peered into the bottom of the wardrobe.

Had Celeste owned so many shoes she'd been able to leave what looked like dozens of pairs behind?

'Maybe they didn't suit the Hollywood lifestyle.' Riley had apparently read his mind because she murmured this explanation while loading Olivia with strappy gold and silver sandals. 'Though…?'

She held up what appeared to be a diamond-encrusted pair and raised her eyebrows.

'Don't say it!' Mitch warned, and the woman had the hide to chuckle.

'Here, pet,' she said to Olivia. 'These will be great to play dress-up! You make sure you keep them with the dresses.'

Olivia's eyes lit up.

'I won't let Mrs Rush pack *these* away,' she declared.

Mitch moved off before he copped more flack for his slackness but, seeing his usually obstreperous daughter so delighted by something as simple as a pair of garish sandals, made him feel old and tired and unbearably sad.

He dumped the clothes on the bed and returned to find Olivia dragging more clothes towards her bedroom.

'She needs ordinary dress-up clothes.' Again Riley answered an unasked question. 'After all, she can't play mother in diamanté sandals and ballgowns.'

'Play mother?' Mitch echoed weakly. What little reality the morning had held was fast slipping beyond his grasp.

'Probably important to her, seeing she hasn't got one,' the woman said, shoving another pile of assorted garments into his arms. 'Although there are enough clothes here to have kept any number of women happy. Was she a compulsive buyer, the S-G?'

'People gave her clothes. Designers. Shops.' Mitch felt compelled to defend the absent Celeste, but the explanation failed to find favour with the visitor who made a ho-ho-hoing kind of noise, as if there might have been something sinister behind the 'gifts'.

Had there been?

As an inner voice asked the question he realised he no longer cared, and the resulting lightness he felt transcended even the hangover.

Momentarily.

'Move!' Riley ordered, taking him by the shoulders and propelling him towards the door. 'I can hear the lads outside so you'll have to finish clearing the room yourself. I'll come back and give you a hand with the bed. You can put it into Olivia's room when you shift hers into your room. Covered with dust sheets, it should be OK.'

He wanted to protest against the orders she was firing at him and to make a firmer point about Olivia shifting—or not shifting—into his bedroom. But Riley Dennison didn't wait for an argument. She'd whisked away, pausing only to take Olivia, who was coming back down the hall, by the hand.

'Come on,' she invited the child. 'If you stay out of the way, you can watch the boys set up their ladders and scaffold.'

Mitch remembered the 'claw hammer coming through

the ceiling' scenario and, with the bundle of clothing pressed to his chest, he hurried after the pair.

'I don't want her out there. Someone could drop something. She could be injured.'

Olivia's lips tightened mutinously, but Riley beat her to the protest.

'I'm not entirely stupid, Dr Hammond. I'll keep hold of her. But as the men are going to be here for the best part of two months, the sooner she meets them the better.'

And without waiting for his reply, or returning his daughter, she strode off, heading for the light truck he now realised was parked in his drive, telling Olivia something about hard hats and the rules of being on a building site.

He gave up, walking slowly towards his bedroom, wondering whether, if he pushed all the clothes to one side of the bed, there'd be enough room for him to crawl in. Just thirty minutes' sleep would make all the difference.

Perhaps when he woke he'd find it had all been a dream.

'I've got a special little hard hat for kids that you can wear whenever you're on the job,' Riley told Olivia.

After hearing the details of this household from her father, she'd been halfway to loving the little girl before she'd arrived. And since meeting her—and the father who referred to his daughter as 'the child'—she'd taken her into her heart.

Fancy having to grow up with a timorous housekeeper, a father who obviously drank too much, if all the signs of a man suffering a mammoth hangover were right, plus the image of a sex-goddess mother in far-away Hollywood.

'This will be your hat while the men are working here.'

She handed Olivia a miniature hard hat which had, in fact, been hers when she'd first started going to jobs with her father.

'At least my mother died,' she murmured to herself, as she tucked the blonde curls out of the way.

Hadyn and Bert were unloading scaffolding but stopped and gravely shook hands with Olivia when Riley introduced her as 'my offsider'.

'Pleased to meet you,' Hadyn said, then he spoke to his 'boss'.

'Are we re-using the tiles or can we throw them off?'

'No to re-using—it's an old house and most of them are cracked and damaged anyway. We're replacing all the tiles when we finish the extension.'

The men exchanged a look of relief. Only a certain number of tiles were ever nailed down, but getting those off without breaking them was a fiddly and time-consuming job.

'And yes to throwing them off. I'll set up the rubbish skip directly under the eaves and I want you to put a safety net around it. Plus one of you standing directly above it when we get to that stage, so you can see where you're throwing. This is an inhabited house and there's a small child involved. I want every precaution taken and safety nets rigged at every stage of the job.'

'Yes, boss!' Bert said, saluting cheekily.

Riley made a growling noise at him and waved him away. The dump truck was just pulling into the drive, delivering the rubbish skip she'd ordered.

'Come on, Olivia. We have to show him where to put it. What window's that one?'

She pointed towards the house and a wide set of windows, trying to place the position off the floor plan.

'That's Daddy's bedroom,' Olivia replied, and a smile twitched around Riley's lips as she waved the truck in that direction.

See if he could sleep off future hangovers with roof tiles or lumps of timber clattering into the metal bin.

'Now, I'm going to have to help the men set up. Do you

want to go inside, or would you like to sit in my truck and watch?'

Olivia favoured the latter option and settled down behind the steering-wheel, where she'd have a good view of what was happening.

Riley checked the vehicle was in park and the tamper-proof lock was working, then she opened the windows and shut the door, leaving the little girl in her dress-circle seat.

Two hours later, they had the scaffolding rigged, a net attached around it to prevent accidentally dropped objects striking an unwary passer-by and a netting chute from the roof to the rubbish skip.

Olivia had lost interest in the process after an hour and Riley had taken her inside, warning her she mustn't come beyond the front porch without an adult.

'As soon as I see you standing there, I'll come and get you,' she'd promised Olivia when she'd been inclined to pout at this decree. 'Look, I'll put a chalk mark on the spot. You stand on the chalk and I'll know you want to come and help.'

She'd dug a piece of chalk out of one of her pockets and drawn a smiley face on the tiles.

The old grump inside would doubtless complain about her defacing his property, but chalk would wash off. And Olivia had stopped pouting.

Now it was time for Riley to face the old grump again. Check that he'd finished clearing out the small bedroom.

Help him move the bed?

He was in the hall beyond the front door, the single bed wedged across the narrow space.

'I told you I'd give you a hand,' Riley reminded him, seizing the mattress and dragging it out of the way so the bed could be tipped on its side.

'Go back in and pull it back a bit, then we'll try it my way.'

Dark eyes, which might be quite attractive when they weren't so bloodshot, darted a murderous glare in her direction, but he did clamber over the bed and ease it away from the wall, then, with no further prompting, helped her turn it on its side.

'No! Not that way—take it into my bedroom. If Olivia has to sleep in there, she can use this bed. Save moving two of them.'

Riley dropped her end. Not a good idea as he then let go of his—and trapped his toe beneath one leg.

She ignored his cries of anguished outrage, and his hopping-up-and-down performance.

'And how well do *you* sleep in a strange bed?' she demanded. 'Olivia's routine is already going to suffer enough disruption with her shifting into your bedroom, so why make things worse by forcing her to sleep in a different bed?'

'I am not forcing her to do anything!' Olivia's father spat the words out, making them sound like metal chips flying from a grinding machine.

He picked up his end and motioned for her to do the same, but when she steered them towards the single bedrooms he didn't argue.

Once they'd manoeuvred the bed into place, Riley looked around and was glad she'd insisted on the swap. Olivia's bed was a pink confection of delight. To put the child into the dreary spare-room bed would have been unkind.

'Now we'll shift this one,' Riley announced. 'Mattress first, don't you think?'

'Oh, am I allowed to think in my own home?' the grump demanded, but he bent and with an ease that belied his distinctly rangy build lifted the mattress and all its frilly covers into his arms.

He squiggled his burden through the door and marched

off down the hall. Riley looked around. The household would have access to the room, so there was no need to shift all the contents, but Olivia might like to have some favourite dolls and books by her bed.

She called the little girl.

'As soon as your dad and I have shifted this bed, do you want to choose some things to take into his room while you're staying there?'

Olivia looked around.

'No, thank you,' she said politely.

'No, thank you? Isn't there a toy you might want to take to bed?'

'No, thank you,' Olivia repeated, then she dashed off again, calling to her father—no doubt organising where they'd put her bed.

The refusal puzzled Riley but she'd have to think about that later. Dr Hammond had returned and they had a bed to shift.

By lunchtime, the men were done. The tiles that would need to be removed were marked and tarpaulins rigged and folded in neat heaps on the roof, ready to be spread over the hole. Eventually, a second storey would rise up through the hole, but until that happened it would be part of Riley's job to make sure the covers were watertight.

Mitch, pleased the activity was finally focussed on the outside of his house, settled in front of the television. Mrs Rush was packing clothes into large plastic envelopes, and Olivia was once again outside with her builder mate. Which left him free to do as he wished.

It was his weekend off and he intended making the most of what was left of it. And that included watching an entire football game.

It was Olivia who interrupted him first.

'Riley wants to see you. She has to switch off the electricity.'

His daughter stumbled over the last word but Mitch understood what she was saying.

Understood it meant the end of Saturday football as well.

'Why the hell does she have to turn off the electricity?' he demanded, then realised he should be yelling at the builder, not his daughter. 'Where is she?'

'Outside!' Olivia led the way.

'I thought you said all you'd do is set things up today,' he stormed, as the cause of all his problems dropped lightly off a ladder and landed in front of him.

'Which we've done,' she said cheerfully. 'But we can't start work on the roof until we've sorted out the power problems.'

She nodded to where a van was pulling into his drive.

'That's the electrician. He'll isolate the wires in that part of the house, perhaps divert some around where we'll be working, and once that's done you won't suffer much disruption at all when the real work begins.'

She gave him a considering look.

'My father did explain it was better to move right out of the house during the renovations, but the idea didn't meet with your approval.'

'So now you're going to make it as difficult as possible for me!' Mitch snarled at her. Then realised he'd snarled and was shaken. Snarling was something he *never* did.

Now Riley Dennison had the hide to smile at him.

'I hardly think going without power for an hour or two will dislocate your life too much. Why don't you do something nice and outdoorsy? Take your daughter to the park. Play on the swings. Clear your head!'

'Oh, could you, Daddy?' Olivia begged before he could snarl some more. 'Can we go to the park? Just you and me?'

She sounded so delighted by what seemed to him like

an exceptionally feeble treat, that he could hardly refuse her.

'OK. Let's get your hat and some sunscreen and tell Mrs Rush what we're doing.'

But he didn't want that woman to think she'd got away with anything, so he glared his disapproval at her before following Olivia into the house.

CHAPTER TWO

RILEY was pleased to see them go. Surely now she could concentrate one hundred percent of her attention on the job.

It was the little girl who'd affected her, she told herself. Not the man with the unshaven chin and red-rimmed eyes and blond, overly long, unruly hair. The little girl reminded her of her own motherless state, though her Dad, the real Riley Dennison, as Dr Snarly Hammond would have said, had more than made up for a loss she'd been too young to understand.

She hurried over to greet the electrician, and explained what she wanted done.

'I assume they've got an earth leakage system installed, with a child in the house,' the man said.

'You'd better check and if not, I'll speak to the owner about putting one in while you're here. It's not much of a cost and although we have one on the power board for our tools, accidents can happen.'

She accompanied him to the meter box, where one look told them the safety device which would shut off power before electrocuting someone in a malfunction hadn't ever been connected.

Darn! It meant seeing him face to face again. She'd hoped to finish her preparatory tasks and not return until shortly before he left for work on Monday morning. And if she was up on the roof at that time, all the better.

She climbed the scaffold to inspect the marked tiles, then, as the carpenters had already left, she stayed up there, high on a ridge, enjoying the wide, sweeping view out to the ocean.

Her father had said the extension—a bedroom, small sitting room and bathroom—was intended for the live-in housekeeper, but Mrs Rush was no longer young, and the stairs might bother her.

Most home-owners would want the view for themselves.

Perhaps Dr Hammond wasn't a view-fancier!

She was musing on this when the electrician came looking for her. Bob James peered upward.

'The hot-water system is in the laundry which is out near the kitchen, so that's no problem,' he called up to her. 'Can I take the power out of the rooms at the far end of the house completely, then rig up electrical cords to the bed lights in the housekeeper's bedroom? I could put in a couple of standard lamps as well, so there's plenty of illumination. It would be safer than trying to run power across the work area to that room and the small bathroom down that end.'

'I can't see any problem with that idea!' she told him. 'I'm coming down now so I'll speak to Mrs Rush.'

She clambered down, and went in to get Mrs Rush's blessing for the plan.

'Doesn't worry me,' Mrs Rush told her. 'In fact, it couldn't be better timed as far as I'm concerned. My daughter's expecting triplets and I'm taking time off to be with her. I could be going any day now.'

Which explained why Olivia could have moved into her room, Riley thought, but sounds outside suggested that the Hammonds were returning and she wanted to get away before she began arguing with him again.

Her emergence from the front door coincided with their arrival.

'Ha! You went to the beach as well,' Riley said to Olivia. 'Sand everywhere. Do you want me to brush it off for you before you go inside?'

'No, thank you,' came the polite reply.

'But it will get on the floor and Mrs Rush will have to clean it up,' Riley reminded her, and received a haughty look for her pains.

But Dr Hammond did catch on, and he knelt to brush sand from the chubby legs.

'Aren't you done yet? And isn't that a different truck in the drive?' he said to Riley, glancing up at her so she noticed his eyes looked slightly better, the toffee-brown colour of the iris now clearly visible and quite attractive.

If brown eyes were your thing!

'That's the electrician.' She began to explain the electrical problem, pleased to get her mind off his eyes, and saw his reaction in an expressive shudder. Grinned to herself. Like most men, he hadn't understood the full implications of having extensive renovation work carried out on his home.

Not that he was home much, according to her father.

Olivia, sand-free now and bored with the conversation, dashed inside, and Riley, remembering the spectacular outlook from the roof and feeling slightly more kindly towards the man after he'd taken Olivia to the park, offered an olive branch.

'Now we've got the scaffolding in place, would you like to climb up and take a look? The new rooms are going to have the best view in the house.'

An expressive grimace told her that the last thing he wanted to do was climb up on his roof.

'Not today, thank you,' he said.

'Hangover got you off balance?' she teased, because he looked as if he could do with some cheering up.

'Certainly not,' he said coldly, and he followed his daughter into the house.

So much for cheering him up! Riley thought, then remembered she hadn't asked him for a key so the workers could come and go when no one was at home.

The door was still ajar. She pushed it open and called his name.

No reply, but from the cacophony of sounds the power was back on. Two television programmes were competing with each other somewhere in the house, and the chances of anyone hearing anything were slim.

She moved further down the hall and was about to call again when a loud crashing noise sent her flying into the small bedroom.

Bob James lay spread-eagled on the floor, broken slabs of plaster and splintered timbers forming an uncomfortable resting place for his inert body.

His lips were blue, although frothy sputum was already drying whitely around them. Riley reacted automatically. She knelt by his side, tipped his head back, checked his mouth for obstructions and started mouth-to-mouth, counting to time the breaths she fed into his body, lifting her head to allow his lungs to collapse and release the air.

She was feeling for a pulse when Dr Hammond arrived.

'Stand clear. I'm a doctor, I'll see to him.'

'Phone an ambulance first. No pulse.'

She measured her hands down the electrician's thick chest and began to pump to get his heart started.

'Phone an ambulance!' she bellowed at the doctor, who'd ignored her first order and had come to squat beside her. 'This will only hold him for a very short time. They have the proper resuscitation equipment.'

He finally departed, but returned seconds later.

'Mrs Rush is phoning. Let me do the chest compressions, you do the breathing. Did he fall? Or was he electrocuted? Are there still live wires somewhere around?'

'No to electrocution. Well, there are no visible burn marks,' Riley told him between sets of breaths. 'Not that I could see. Anyway, he'd already turned off the power from this end of the house. He must have been up there taping the wires out of the way.'

She frowned, thinking things through.

'He's used to clambering around on and under a roof, so I doubt it was a simple fall. More likely a heart attack, given that he's grossly overweight and the only exercise he ever gets is climbing up and down a ladder.'

'He could have had it somewhere other than in my roof!' Dr Hammond said, although his compressions were as even and consistent as any Riley had ever seen. Firm hands and long, slender fingers, but with a strength in them...

'If we keep him alive I'll be sure to tell him how inconvenient it was!' she retorted, hoping conversation might divert her mind from its random observations. 'But although this wasn't an electrical accident, I think you should have whoever replaces him as electrician put an earth leakage system on your power outlets, so accidents can't happen in the future. I'd have thought a doctor with a child would have insisted on it being done before the baby could walk.'

He gave her a look that would have shrivelled a lesser person, but Riley was used to men's reactions to her often unasked-for advice, and she grinned unrepentantly.

His only reaction was to pretend he hadn't heard, and count louder the beats they needed for their timing.

'He's got a pulse,' Dr Hammond said several minutes later, his voice betraying a sense of victory which Riley shared.

A vehicle pulling up outside told them help was at hand, and when the two ambulance officers came into the small room, carrying the cases she knew held life-support equipment, she gratefully withdrew.

Then had second thoughts. OK, so the guy was a doctor, but was he thinking straight today?

And he probably knew no more than Bob's name—if he

remembered that. Someone would have to give patient details.

She eased back in, keeping well out of the way as the men began work, moving as efficiently as a well-trained dance team, checking Bob's airway, using a tube to maintain it during transport, fitting an oxygen mask, inserting a wide-bore catheter, pumping one of the thrombolytic agents into his blood to disperse the clots. Or would it be sodium bicarbonate? Would they give stronger drugs before learning his medical history?

Dr Hammond was standing against the opposite wall, and from the look on his face he was finding the proceedings as fascinating as she was.

'What's that?' he asked, as a small machine was introduced.

'Heart monitor,' the attendant told him, opening Bob's shirt and attaching electrodes. 'Probably smaller than you're used to seeing at the hospital, Doc. It's a new mobile unit. Our equipment is getting more and more compact. See here!'

He lifted another box, barely larger than a child's small schoolbag.

'New hands-off defibrillator. We'll have it open and ready in case we lose him again on the trip. With the limited space in the ambulance cabin, we need all the help we can get.'

The second attendant was completing the necessary paperwork, then he began securing the tubes and wires.

'Another ambulance is here,' Mrs Rush announced, poking her head through the door then withdrawing it very hastily.

'That's our transport,' an attendant said. 'We're the advance team. We just get him ready.'

Get him ready?

The thought of Bob being shifted reminded Riley of something else.

'He fell through the ceiling,' she told the attendants. 'Landed on his back. He could have spinal injuries as well, so make sure you brace him before you lift him.'

The attendants nodded, but Dr Hammond sent a questioning look her way. No doubt thinking she'd butted in again for no good reason.

She was glad when the stretcher-bearers arrived and she had to leave the room so they could get in.

Out in the hall, she pulled off the scarf she'd twisted around her hair what seemed like days and days ago, then ran her fingers through the tangled skeins. She'd have to phone Bob's wife, but only when she knew what hospital the ambulance would choose. Port Anderson Private was the closest, but the public hospital might have better facilities for heart-attack victims. She'd been away from town for too long to know.

Dr Hammond came out of the room, followed by the attendants wheeling their patient, who was now rigged up with tubes and mask, and wired to the monitoring device.

'They're taking him to the public hospital. Do you know his family? Will you contact them?'

The doctor seemed to do a double take, as if he'd just noticed whom he was addressing, then gathered himself and spoke again.

'You can tell them he's OK—not in immediate danger.' There was a pause before he added, 'Thanks mainly to your prompt action.'

The praise embarrassed Riley and she shrugged it off.

'You were there just as quickly.'

She pulled her father's mobile out of her pocket and walked towards the front door, checking the list of pre-set codes pasted on the back which would give her the button to press to connect her to the electrician's house.

Mrs James took the news badly. Or maybe, Riley decided, she'd delivered it badly.

'I'll come and get you,' she soothed the frantic woman. 'Drive you to the hospital.'

You should have done that in the first place, she told herself as she dug her car keys out of another pocket and jogged towards her father's vehicle. You're not thinking straight.

Not thinking at all! she realised hours later when Bob had been pronounced out of danger and other family members had turned up to hold Mrs James's hand.

An image of the man as he'd lain on the floor had been niggling at her mind since she'd first seen him there, and she'd put it down to shock.

But there had been something more. The shattered pieces of timber. Bob had been in the space between the ceiling and the tiles, presumably moving around on the top of the rafters. When he'd collapsed, the rafters should have held him, not splintered and given way so he'd come crashing through the ceiling.

Riley sighed and headed back to Dr Hammond's house. She'd be the last person he wanted to see.

It was Saturday night. Maybe he was out on a hot date.

She sighed again. How long since she'd had a hot date?

Any date, in fact?

But once at the house, the sight of the doctor's car tucked snugly into the carport suggested he wasn't out at all.

She considered her options. She was tired, dirty and quite possibly on the nose after a hectic day on the job and the hours at the hospital. He wouldn't want to see her, and she definitely didn't want to see him. Or have him see her, looking as she was, if it came to that. A girl had some pride!

All she needed to do was check the roof. The bit over the spare bedroom which was now off limits to the family.

If she lifted a few tiles...

She grabbed a torch from the glove-box and opened the car door, pushing it not quite shut so the light went out but no noise would alert the family to her presence.

Then she crossed to the scaffolding and swung effortlessly up, pausing, as her head came clear of the netting, to look out at a moon-washed ocean.

'You were right. It's a great view, isn't it?' a voice said, and she shrieked with fright, grasping at the scaffold to prevent herself plummeting back down to the ground.

'What are you doing up here?' she demanded, when she'd recovered her breath and her heart had stopped pounding enough to allow her to speak.

'It's my roof,' Dr Hammond said calmly.

'But you didn't want to climb up earlier,' she reminded him.

'So?' he said, and when she didn't answer added, 'Now perhaps you'll tell me what *you're* doing here. Snooping around like a burglar casing the joint.'

'Casing the joint indeed!' Riley snorted. 'What's that? A line from a movie you've seen?'

'I thought it was the correct terminology,' her companion said. 'Not that I've had many dealings with members of the burglary profession.' He was looking out towards the sea as he spoke, but now he turned to where she hovered at the top of the scaffolding. 'But we're discussing your presence on my roof, not my language.'

The ball was back in Riley's court, but she was reluctant to hit it. Reluctant to worry him with more bad news if what she feared was right.

Perhaps she could just sit on the roof and admire the view. Pretend it was what she'd come to see?

And have him think her crazy?

'I just wanted to check on…' she hesitated while she thought of something that might sound feasible '…whether the tarpaulins were weighted down.'

'They are,' the doctor told her. 'Though why you'd want them up here before the tiles come off, I haven't figured.'

She considered not explaining, then decided he was paying for the job so she told him how tiles were sometimes cracked while the men were marking them and setting up ready for the job.

'And if that happens, it's easier to have the tarps on the roof ready to cover any leaking tiles should a storm blow up.'

Though this was true enough, it didn't get her into the space between the ceiling and the tiles, which was where she'd been heading.

'I'd better have a look myself,' Riley said, to make her explanation seem believable.

And silently she added, Then get out of here, as the effect of the moon and the view and possibly not having eaten for hours made chatting with this man on his roof seem an enticing way to spend a Saturday evening.

Or what was left of it.

Which was ridiculous, given that she hadn't liked what she'd seen or heard of him so far.

Torch in hand, she made her way to where the tarps were folded. The men *had* weighted them down efficiently, which was to be expected, but her problem remained.

Time to take another tack.

'Could I go inside to check the damage in the small bedroom?' she asked him. 'I've a ladder on the truck. It won't take me long.'

He didn't reply but as he left his perch and began to descend, she took it as agreement and followed him down. Then lost an argument over who'd carry the ladder into the house.

'I realise this is very chivalrous of you, but it's my job to carry it,' she protested, trotting mutinously along behind him and the ladder.

The second bedroom was dark, and Riley turned on her torch, telling him where to position the ladder so she could see up into the rafters.

Though she didn't need to climb it. A closer look at the splintered wood still scattered on the carpet told her what she feared was true.

'Damn!' she muttered to herself, and then, out of sympathy for the man who in the torchlight looked as weary as she felt, she climbed the ladder and shone the torch around as if she'd noticed nothing untoward at all.

Bad news didn't get worse with keeping, and if she announced the presence of termites in his house right here and now he'd not be able to sleep, imagining he could hear them chomping through the boards above his head.

And it could be dry rot, not termites. She'd have to take a piece of the shattered rafter home and have her father check it out.

'OK, I've seen enough,' she announced, climbing back down and coming face to face with the man who was holding the ladder steady.

Then, because he was giving her a considering kind of scrutiny, and she remembered how dirty and dishevelled she was, she added a lame, 'Thanks!' And stepped away, snapping off the torch and plunging the room into darkness.

Not a good idea. She turned it back on but pointed the beam away from them.

'If it was a fall, not a heart attack, does he sue you or me? Who's liable?'

'It was a heart attack,' Riley assured him, chuckling to herself that she'd taken the look as a personal appraisal, not a professional assessment of how things stood. 'I waited long enough for tests to confirm it.'

She pushed past him to the door, then remembered she wanted a sample of the timber and bent to collect some pieces.

'Kindling for a fire? Waste not, want not?'

Here she was, all consideration for his welfare, and as a reward she had to put up with him deliberately needling her.

'Do you want some more? There are any number of pieces here on the floor.'

He was plucking them off the carpet—holding them out towards her—the brown eyes alight with mockery.

Forget consideration for his welfare!

'No, I don't want any more,' she snapped. So much for trying to protect him! 'What I have is more than enough to check on whether dry rot or termites have eaten through your rafters. And rather than being facetious, you'd be better off working out if you can afford to build your extensions *and* replace your entire roof, and quite possibly most of the walls as well.'

She stormed down the corridor to the front door, then, hearing his footsteps behind her, she swung around again.

'I'll be back in the morning. Early. Probably with a dog!' she announced.

Mitch heard these final words, but they didn't make any more sense than her earlier pronouncement had. He groaned and held his head in his hands. Time and the fresh air in the park had cured his hangover, but the events of the day had been so bizarre that some kind of waking dream seemed the most likely explanation.

Dry rot? Termites? Replacing the entire roof?

And where did the dog come into it?

He walked through to the living room and sank down into his favourite chair. Time to sort out what was bothering him most.

An image of a tall, slim woman in overalls came immediately to mind.

No! It couldn't be a sexist thing! He had no problems with female doctors, or male nurses, so why would a female builder bother him? From the little he'd seen, she was efficient, and she'd certainly reacted well to the crisis.

He took another look at the mental picture and saw the hair.

Yep! She was certainly a more likely builder when that abundant mass of russet curls was tied up in a scarf. Builders came in all shapes and sizes, but none he'd seen had ever had such hair!

Not that hair should decrease her ability to do her job.

Most people had hair.

He had too much of it himself at present. Really should find time to get it cut.

He rested his head back against the cushioned support and closed his eyes. He should be thinking about dry rot or—heaven forbid—termites. Not russet curls that had glowed like fire in the moonlight and flickered with a thousand tiny flames in the torch's beam.

The excited barking of a dog awoke him, and he jerked upright, then slumped back into the chair as every muscle in his body protested over the way he'd slept.

'Riley's here and she's got a dog!' his daughter, who had apparently been standing by the chair, waiting for him to wake, informed him. 'He's a sniffer dog.'

'Sniffer dog? What's she looking for? Illicit drugs? What does she think this place is? Open house? And what's she doing here at this hour of a Sunday morning?'

From the look on Olivia's face he must be shouting, so he lowered the pitch of his voice an octave, and the volume several decibels.

'And what are you doing out of bed so early?' he asked, bending to lift his daughter for a quick hug and kiss.

'Riley says us builders always start early,' Olivia told him, and Mitch felt a stab of annoyance.

Was 'Riley says' going to become a catch-cry in the house?

Which brought him back to what Riley was doing here.

She'd told him something last night. And, yes, she'd mentioned a dog, but his mind had been mesmerised by that damn hair and he'd lost track of what was what.

He made his way, stiffly, to the front door, where the woman waited patiently, a golden cocker spaniel straining at his leash.

Fortunately the hair was today tucked under a cap, and with the slim figure clad in the familiar overalls she had the look of a woman concerned solely with business.

'Another rough night?' she asked, tell-tale little wrinkles appearing at the corners of her unusual eyes as she pretended she wasn't laughing at him.

'I fell asleep in the chair!' he told her, then told himself he shouldn't have answered as it was none of her business how he spent his nights.

'Happens!' she said, then she waved her hand towards the dog. 'The wood I took home has been eaten through by termites. There were none actually in it, and the damage could be old, but this is Dave. He's a sniffer dog. Trained to detect any sites of current activity.'

'Sites of current activity?' Mitch muttered weakly. 'I was hoping at least that part of yesterday had been something I'd dreamed. Sites, plural? There could be more? Termites still eating through my house? The walls as well as the rafters?'

He flung his arms in the air.

'I can't handle this. I should have sold. Bought something bigger. Bugger the view and convenience.'

He looked hopefully at the woman who was still standing on his doorstep.

'You haven't taken any tiles off the roof. I could still sell!'

She gave him a sardonic look.

'Most intelligent buyers have an expert check for termites before they sign a contract. Your chances of selling the place, if it is infested, are zilch! Now, if you've finished complaining, may we get started? I don't particularly want to waste an entire Sunday sorting out your problems.'

He stepped back and waved her to come in. Intelligent buyers indeed! How was she to know he hadn't taken that precaution? For all she knew the termite invasion could have been recent. *Since* an inspection.

Although he couldn't remember if he had insisted on one...

'Where do you want to start?' he demanded.

'In the bathrooms!'

He might have guessed. He wanted only to escape to his bathroom and have a shower and shave. Get into clean clothes. Feel normal again.

'Come and do Daddy's first,' Olivia suggested, and before Mitch could protest, the woman and the dog were following his daughter as she danced blithely down the hall.

He should make himself a coffee, but the need to use a bathroom suggested that wasn't a good idea, so he tagged along and arrived in time to see the dog go berserk, barking and scratching at the tiles beside his shower alcove.

With absolutely no regard for his belongings, Riley Dennison took a chisel from her pocket and broke the tile away, then a few more tiles within the alcove itself and a few more. The dog became overly excited, and Olivia, joining in the fun, began to jump up and down.

'Look, Daddy, look! Hundreds and hundreds of ants. Riley says if you're very quiet you can hear their little feet walking up and down inside the walls. Do you think we'll hear them tonight?'

Mitch closed his eyes and prayed for patience. This couldn't really be happening to him, could it?

Riley Dennison looked up from where she crouched on the floor.

'Do you want me to track them down? Find where they are and where they've been? It will mean stripping the lining away from a lot of walls and then repairing the rotten timber.'

He imagined he could see sympathy in her lovely eyes, but guessed it could just as well be delight at his predicament.

'Do we exterminate them first?'

She nodded. 'I know a good fumigator. He can do a thorough inspection and give you a quote for exterminating them and setting up some kind of system to discourage their return.'

'Discourage?' Mitch stormed as the scenario grew more grim by the moment. 'Can't he get rid of them for ever?'

Riley eased herself to her feet, and looked directly into his eyes.

'There are no guarantees with termites, but you can buy a certain amount of protection. Having regular inspections is the best insurance against it happening again.

'Well?' she added, into a silence Mitch hadn't noticed. He'd actually been thinking how refreshing it was to meet a woman whose eyes were almost on a level with his. Most women looked up to him, literally, not figuratively, of course. But this one—

'Well, what?'

She gave him an exasperated look. 'Do you want me to arrange for someone to come? The chap's name is Michael Wren. He can give you scads of references. Actually,

Dave's his dog. I borrowed him. Michael's one of the first
people in Port to use a dog for this work.'

She waved her hand to where Olivia was patting and
petting the animal—and accepting totally unhygienic kisses
from an animal whose last tongue contact had been with
termites.

'Olivia likes him, doesn't she? Does she have a pet?
Perhaps she needs a dog. My Labrador's just had puppies.
I've sold a couple of them but there's one gentle wee thing
would make a perfect pet for a little girl.'

Mitch shook his head. His life was reeling out of control.
He had cracked tiles on his roof, termites were eating his
walls, and this woman was talking about puppies.

And Olivia, who'd obviously heard the conversation, was
jumping up and down and yelling, 'May I, Daddy? May I
have a dog?'

He was about to snap an abrupt no at his only child when
he remembered exactly how such a definite refusal would
be received. Olivia might be over the accepted tantrum-
throwing age of two, but she could still win any tantrum-
throwing contest hands down.

She'd inherited all her mother's dramatic talent, and right
now he had neither the strength nor the patience to endure
the performance.

He used the old fall-back of all parents.

'We'll see,' he said, but he frowned ferociously at Riley
Dennison as he said it. If she was going to continue to
supervise in her father's place, he'd have to have a talk to
her about where her job began and ended.

He'd make it clear that putting stupid ideas into his
daughter's head went way beyond the boundaries.

Way, way beyond.

CHAPTER THREE

'Do you have a manhole in your bedroom?'

'What's a manhole?' Olivia was easily diverted from the puppy decision.

'A hole in the ceiling so a man—or these days even a woman—can crawl up into the roof.'

'Then why aren't they called woman-holes?' Olivia demanded.

Mitch shook his head. Even without a hangover he was having trouble with the conversations going on around him.

'Why do you need a manhole?' he demanded, cutting in before the woman-hole thing took precedence in the builder's mind.

'So I can have a look at the rafters in this section of the house. See how much damage has been done up there. I might need to get a structural engineer to OK the building before I let the men back to work.'

'Will you take Dave up into the roof?' Olivia asked, but Mitch was too busy handling the concept of structural engineers to worry about a dog in the ceiling.

'Just keep out of this for a minute,' he said to Olivia.

Well, OK, he might have snapped it rather than saying it.

Whatever he'd done, it had the predictable result, for his daughter was now bellowing loudly, the dog was barking, the white ants, no doubt, were considering leaving his tasty timbers for a quieter life in a lunatic asylum.

Riley Dennison, of course, was laughing.

Not just chuckling. Or making any attempt to hide her

mirth. There she was, holding her sides and gasping for air. That kind of laughing!

'Stop the noise, the lot of you!' he roared, effectively silencing the dog and the builder but making Olivia worse.

Then, as he contemplated running away from home as the only possible option left to him, Riley took over.

'That's enough, Olivia,' she said, squatting beside the little girl and speaking quietly but firmly. 'I can't possibly give a puppy to someone who makes so much noise. The poor little thing would be frightened to death, hearing you go on like that.'

The noise stopped abruptly and tear-drenched blue eyes looked wonderingly at Riley.

'Really? I'd frighten the puppy? Don't puppies like noise?'

'They hate it,' Riley told her. 'Even bigger dogs are frightened by loud noises. You heard how Dave barked when you began to cry.'

Olivia looked from Riley to the dog, then up at her father, who was having trouble believing this miraculous cessation of noise.

'I won't be able to cry if I have a puppy?' she asked, and Mitch knew he'd lost one argument but had possibly gained far more than that.

He, too, knelt, so he was on eye level with his daughter.

'Only very quietly if it's something important to you,' he said gently, then he took her in his arms and kissed the tears away.

But knowing Olivia, this transformation wouldn't last. He wouldn't prostrate himself in gratitude to Riley Dennison just yet.

'I guess we're going to have to take a look at your puppies,' he said instead, and saw the hint of a smile sparkle in her eyes.

Like water in an alpine stream—that was the nearest he could come to describing the colour and the clarity.

'Now, Daddy? Can we go now?'

Olivia's question reminded him it was no time to be thinking of his builder's eye colour, although the eyes themselves were mesmerising him.

'Wasn't there something else you had to do here?' he muttered, unable to believe he'd completely lost track of the situation.

'Manholes. The roof,' she said helpfully. 'I need to take a look.' Then she straightened up but added to Olivia, 'I'll be home late this afternoon if it suits your dad to bring you over then to see the puppies. Now, why don't you go and talk to Mrs Rush about getting one? She might have a box you can make into a bed for it.'

'But what about the house?' Mitch demanded, when Olivia had trotted happily away to discuss dog bedding. 'You're talking structural engineers. If we have to move out, we can't take a dog. I know I agreed, but—'

Riley turned to face him. Good-looking he might be. And from all accounts, he was a good doctor. But as a father? What was he thinking, allowing a four-year old to throw tantrums like the one they'd just witnessed?

She reminded herself that his child-rearing activities were none of her business, and answered the question he'd asked.

'Unless the place needs to be condemned, which I very much doubt as Dad did have a quick look in the ceiling when he first gave a quote, you won't have to move out. It might be inconvenient for a while, but you'll manage.'

'I guess I'll have to,' he said gloomily. 'With school holidays coming up, any rental accommodation will be booked solid. The joys of living in a resort town!'

'Oh, please!' Riley groaned. 'Enough of this negativity! So you've a few termites in your house! So what?'

She flung out her arms then saw the rage building in his eyes, and, too late, wondered if she'd gone too far!

'A few termites in my house?' he roared. 'I've my roof about to come off, and you're talking about pulling out of the job because it might be unsafe. Then there's the interesting thought that, if I'm very quiet, I can listen to the happy patter of termite feet as they run riot in my timbers. And you think I'm being negative?'

The sheer volume of his voice started the dog barking again, and Olivia reappeared on cue.

'Daddy, you're frightening the dog!' she said, and Riley hid a smile as the infuriated man bit back a bellow of unadulterated rage and flung away from them, down the hall and out of the front door. From the way he was moving, she doubted if he'd stop until he reached the beach—and possibly the ocean.

Maybe the winter waves would be enough to cool him off.

Olivia ran as far as the door then turned tearfully back to Riley, who scooped her up and gave her a comforting hug.

'He's a little upset over the termites,' she explained, 'but he'll be back soon.'

Once Olivia had been sufficiently reassured, Riley retrieved her ladder from the small bedroom and carried it down the hall to where she'd located a manhole.

Common sense suggested she check the rafters and get out of the house before Dr Hammond returned. She seemed to have the knack of upsetting him.

Mitch strode along the beach, feeling the chill wind cool his blood, and lower his heart rate. That damned woman might mock his reaction to the disaster, but she only knew the half of it.

His mind shifted to work-related thoughts.

Peter Sutton's imminent departure—to take up a study scholarship overseas—had not only left his loosely structured group one child psychologist short, but had thrust the professionals who worked out of his building back into the old argument of whether they needed such a person at all.

He'd been half-hearted about renting space to Peter originally, thinking two Obstetric and Gynaecology specialists, two paediatricians, an occupational therapist and a physiotherapist in the building were enough to provide a good cover of services to young families. A dentist who specialised in children's oral health had been one option he'd considered for the final suite of rooms, but Peter had been a friend of a friend and Mitch had been persuaded to let him take the space.

Since then, Peter's success with some of their patients had been so great Mitch now believed there was a real need within what they considered their 'group' for a child psychologist. And to keep the person to whom Peter was passing on his patients made sense.

Yet, to be fair, Mitch felt he had to consult the other professionals who already rented rooms in the building. Though they all worked independently, they covered for each other and referred to each other, giving them a group dynamic as well as individual practices. As one of the O and G specialists, his contact with the babies he delivered ended at the six-week check-up. It was the two paediatricians who would have more to do with Peter's replacement.

Which *was* his problem! The two paediatricians were both excellent doctors, but agree on anything?

Not in this lifetime!

If one agreed it would be good to have Peter's replacement in the building with them, the other would disagree on principle.

Then there was Tracey, the occupational therapist, who, since the announcement of Peter's departure, had been bad-gering Mitch to allow her to switch to his rooms because they were more spacious.

But she didn't want to pay the extra rent.

'Who'd be a landlord?' he muttered at the pair of oyster-catchers who were tiptoeing delicately along the edge of the surf.

Perhaps he wouldn't consult at all. Make the decision himself and tell them that's how it would be. Sign a lease with the new person. Though having had his official fare-well, Peter wasn't leaving for a fortnight. Mitch could meet his replacement and then decide. Peter had already given him some info about the person—enthusiastic info—but the details were hazy.

He reached the great humps of rock that stood out on Sunrise Beach, and turned to stride back again, his mind, having made a decision about the replacement, now return-ing to termites and his extension.

To the woman who had tripled the chaos in his life.

'Trust a woman!' he muttered, although he knew it was unfair to blame her or her entire sex for his termites.

Perhaps if he faced up to one problem at a time. He hadn't exactly given her the go-ahead to get an extermi-nator in. Do that first, and think about the rest later.

Relieved to have even this much of a plan, he headed back up to the house and was about to walk straight in when he remembered Riley admonishing Olivia about the sand on her legs.

He slipped off his sandy shoes and started down the hall, but his eyes hadn't quite adjusted from bright sunlight to gloom so he hit the ladder just as the woman he'd been thinking about started down the rungs.

Somehow he managed to catch her, and hold her, sway-ing under the weight. But as the ladder went over he went with it, hitting the wall before they ended in a tangle of metal and limbs, the warm softness of a female body pressed weightily on top of him.

'I'm so sorry,' she said. A confusing remark, given that it had been he who'd knocked the ladder out from under her feet. 'Are you all right?'

She lifted herself high enough off him to look down into his face and her fingers, soft but firm, moved in his hair.

'Did you hit your head?'

For once she wasn't yelling at him—or laughing at him. The thought made him sigh, and his body responded to the womanly concern, but as she tried to untangle herself the ladder twisted around and clipped him on the ear, and the momentary rapport he'd felt with Riley Dennison vanished.

'I'm fine,' he assured her. He sat up straight, moved the ladder, propped his back against the wall, shrugged his shoulder in an attempt to ease the pain in his neck, reassured Olivia, who'd appeared with the dog, and waved Mrs Rush, who'd managed to avoid most of the morning's chaos, away. 'Just fine!'

Olivia began to chuckle.

'You did look funny, all tangled in the ladder with Riley on top of you.'

He'd felt funny, too, but he wasn't going to tell anyone that bit! Instead, he grinned at his daughter.

'I'm glad it made you laugh,' he said.

Then, finally, he looked at Riley, who'd also sat up, her back propped against the opposite wall.

Not laughing, but looking at him with a puzzled frown knitting the clear pale skin between her eyebrows. Somewhere in the action her cap had come off, so the russet hair again tumbled around her shoulders, making her skin even paler and her eyes strangely luminous.

'The rafters and beams above your bedroom are sound and I can't see any evidence of damaged timbers anywhere but where Bob crashed through,' she said, but the words sounded far away, as if echoing down a tunnel.

'Oh, heavens, he did bang his head,' he heard someone say, then the nightmare he'd been enduring turned into a pleasant dream. He was high in the mountains by an alpine stream, and a woman with long russet curls was floating over the grass towards him, clad in nothing but diamond-encrusted sandals.

'Come on, Mitch, get with it!'

Male voice, not female!

He opened his eyes and looked around. Pale green walls, no, not walls, curtains. A sensation of activity beyond them. Brett Walters peering anxiously down at him.

Brett Walters?

What was a neurosurgeon doing here?

And where was here?

'What's happening?' he asked, though the words came out more garbled than he'd intended.

'What do you remember?'

So much for getting a straight answer from a doctor!

'A woman in diamond sandals?'

'That's it? Nothing else?' his friend demanded.

'Well, I couldn't see her clearly, but I fancy she was naked,' Mitch told him.

'I don't want to know about your fantasies!' Brett said crossly. 'What do you remember about the accident?'

Mitch tried to think.

'There was a ladder. Did I fall off the roof?'

'The ladder's close,' Brett told him. 'Don't worry, the rest will come. My guess is you jarred your neck and moved the bones out of alignment sufficiently to put pressure on your carotid.'

'Pressure on my carotid doesn't sound a very medically correct term, mate,' Mitch told him. 'Left or right, for a start? And what do you mean, you're guessing? Don't you know?'

'No! But from what I've heard that's what could have happened. Either that, or you passed out through pain. Your right shoulder was dislocated as well. Fortunately, that gorgeous redhead you were fooling around with had enough sense to get help fast.'

Mitch recalled ambulance personnel racing into his house, a memory he'd dismissed earlier as being connected to another accident. He was trying to retrieve more information when Brett continued.

'Fred Groves did a manipulation under a very light anaesthetic to get your shoulder back in place, then handed you over to me. I did scans and X-rays while we had you out to it. I can't see anything disastrous but you're to keep your neck in the hard collar for a week—no argument on that point.'

Mitch raised his hand to his neck, felt the rigid collar and groaned with frustration.

'And keep your arm in a sling as much as possible for the next few days to help heal the traumatised tendons in your shoulder. Two days off, doctor's orders, and after that, providing you can accommodate the collar, you can go back to work.'

No doubt Brett was talking sense, but Mitch's brain, refusing to accept this talk of collars and days off work, had made its way back to the 'gorgeous redhead you were fooling around with' phrase!

'What gorgeous redhead?' he demanded.

Brett laughed.

'Come on, mate! Don't give me the old amnesia routine. Five-ten, and slim, but curvy in all the right places. Hair that's begging to have fingers run through it. Utterly delightful creature. Where did you find her? Not here in Port, that's for sure!'

'You don't mean Riley Dennison, do you?' Mitch asked weakly.

Surely he couldn't be beholden to that aggravating woman? Owe his life, or at least his brain function, to her?

'That's the one! She's outside now. Olivia was with her, but Clare, your secretary, came in and took her home to play with her kids. Riley thought it was better for Olivia not to see you lying on a hospital gurney.'

'Riley thought...' Mitch muttered. 'Why's she making decisions for my daughter? Where's Mrs Rush? Don't tell me she's in hospital as well?'

Again Brett laughed.

'Well, actually, she is,' he said, obviously delighted at having more bad news to impart. 'Though not this one and just visiting. Her daughter's gone into labour. The triplets are arriving. She's left for Coffs Harbour. According to Riley, Mrs Rush said she told you to organise her replacement months ago, but apparently—'

Mitch waved his hands at him.

'Don't tell me any more. I refuse to listen. And you can stop that guffawing. I've known times when your life was a mess.'

He paused, remembering the termites, and in all fairness added, 'But not quite as bad a mess as I'm in now.'

He closed his eyes. If he went back to sleep, could he recapture the meadow scene? Though he'd prefer a dark-haired woman this time. First a blonde and now a redhead, tormenting him even in his dreams!

'Don't go to sleep. You're out of here, mate. There's no sign of any fracture in the bones, no obvious problem, and no reason why you can't go home. You'll probably sleep better in your own bed.'

Was that an echo of another conversation or was he hearing double?

He was considering this when Brett pulled back the curtains to reveal a frowning Riley Dennison hovering just beyond them.

She shook her head, as if disappointed to see him still alive.

'Heavens, but you can get yourself into sticky situations!' she said, but there was a tension in her teasing words which puzzled him. 'Are you always this disaster-prone, or have the planets lined up against you this month? Perhaps the Sex Goddess has a voodoo doll and is sticking pins in it.'

Mitch struggled into a sitting position and glared at the woman.

'Go away!' he said. 'Go right away.'

She grinned at him.

'OK, I'll take back the Sex Goddess thing. That was a low blow when you're already down and have so recently been out. But don't be too hasty to send me away. I'm here to give you a lift home.'

'I'd rather walk than get in a car with you!' Mitch told her. 'You think *I'm* disaster-prone. Look at the cause! Take a look at yourself. You come banging into my life and everything goes to hell! *You're* the disaster area! You should wear a warning sign—'

Riley Dennison held up her hands.

'OK! I get the message. But if you're walking home, I'd start now if I were you. I told Clare you'd be home by five-thirty. She won't want to drop Olivia off at an empty house.'

She turned away, but Mitch had recovered sufficient balance to lurch to his feet and grab her arm.

'Empty house? Where's Mrs Rush?'

Riley shook her head.

'Boy, you *are* confused. Or do you just not listen to anything you don't want to hear?'

Mitch resisted an urge to shake her, instead growling out his defence. 'I heard you tell me about the termites.'

'Ah, but you saw them, too,' she countered, then she cocked her head and looked straight into his eyes. 'I heard Dr Walters tell you about the triplets. And apparently Mrs Rush has been telling you for months that she'd be leaving just as soon as her daughter went into labour. She even offered to advertise for someone to replace her for the three months she would be taking off. But, no, you said you'd handle it, and filed it away in some dark recess of your mind where all unwanted decisions must be tucked.'

As the enormity of this new disaster dawned, Mitch slumped back onto the gurney.

'The triplets aren't due for months!' he muttered weakly.

'And you, an obstetrician, have never heard of multiple babies arriving early?'

Her sarcasm scorched across his skin.

'I do have other things on my mind,' he retorted.

'More important than your daughter's welfare?' Riley hit right back at him, and Mitch, realising what she'd said was true, shuddered.

'I need a wife,' he muttered. 'Someone who can handle some of these decisions.'

'Join the club,' Riley told him heartlessly. 'I've thought that for years. Working and studying. Worrying about Dad. And still having to shop and cook and remember people's birthdays. I've often thought how good men had it, being able to leave so much of the everyday stuff in their lives to a wife.'

She gave him an enigmatic smile.

'Not that most men appreciate just how essential she is—until it's too late.'

'That's a very cynical attitude,' Mitch said crossly, though in truth, *he'd* never realised how smoothly his home life had run until Celeste had taken off for Hollywood and he'd had to fend not only for himself but for a year-old daughter as well. True, Mrs Rush had been there even then, but it had been Celeste who'd told the housekeeper what to do, who'd planned meals, arranged her days off and generally organised things for everyone.

And had still found time to work—to learn lines, rehearse and commute to Sydney or the Gold Coast for parts in TV shows and movies.

A sigh heaved up from deep within him.

'Come on,' Riley said, and her voice was gentle now. 'I'll run you home. You look done in.'

Too confused to argue, he stood up and let her hold his arm as she steered him out of the big emergency area and across the car park towards her truck.

'No dog?' he asked as she opened the passenger door for him.

'No, I dropped Dave back with his owner and arranged for a full inspection to take place tomorrow. I can put it off if you're not up to it.'

Mitch shuddered.

'I will never be up to it,' he told her, 'but I guess tomorrow will be as good a day as any to hear more bad news.'

Riley chuckled.

'It mightn't be all bad,' she said, her voice even more soothing than the words.

'Mightn't it?' Mitch growled, but he didn't add a sarcastic 'with you around?' because suddenly it was very comforting to have Riley Dennison taking care of him.

Well, *someone* taking care of him.

It was the 'taking care of' part that appealed.

Wasn't it?

CHAPTER FOUR

THE ladder was still blocking the hall, and Riley went ahead to move it. Then, suddenly ill at ease in this new and undefined role of chief attendant to an injured man, she decided briskness was the answer.

'You go straight through to bed,' she told Mitch. 'Can you get undressed on your own?'

He cast her a look of loathing that outdid anything he'd directed at her thus far. And there'd been some beauties!

But at least he obeyed, heading directly to his bedroom, where an anguished cry only minutes later suggested he might not be able to manage.

She hurried into the room.

He had been able to remove his shirt, but it had only been half on, one side across his bad shoulder and the sling he was supposed to wear for a few days.

'It's the stupid brace. I can't look down. Surely I can take it off occasionally.'

'Brett said you had to keep it on for twenty-four hours, and after that you can take it off to shower and put it straight back afterwards. Shall I run a bath for you?'

'I can run my own bath,' he grumped at her. 'That's if I ever get out of these trousers.'

Riley had been so busy surreptitiously checking out his bare chest that she hadn't caught on to the problem. Which, from the way his fingers were working frantically at the material of his trousers, was a stuck zipper.

'Here, let me do it,' she said, and stepped forward.

The movement caused her 'patient' to leap hurriedly backwards, muttering, 'You stay away from me!'

It was a threat that would have had more oomph if the bed hadn't been in the way. It hit him behind the knees and he tumbled back onto it.

'Oh, don't be so pathetic!' Riley told him, advancing with a determination she was far from feeling. 'I'm not about to violate your person, or take advantage of you in your injured state!'

Act cool, she told herself. Fix the problem and get out.

And if you dare blush! she added to her fair and unreliable skin. If you so much as dare to go even slightly pink…

She moved his hands, grasped the metal tab and wiggled it.

It was very stuck.

She tried to yank it back up, but force wasn't going to work.

Beneath her ministrations, Mitch had gone very still.

And very silent.

'I'll just get a coat-hanger,' she told him, careful not to meet his eyes in case the blushing-thing got going.

He shot upright again, clutching protectively at his clothing.

'A coat hanger? What are you going to do to me now?'

She opened a closet and smelt the maleness of it. So different to a woman's space. Found an empty hanger and crossed back to the bed.

'I don't particularly like the connotations of that question. Makes it sound as if I'm responsible for all your problems.' Riley waved the hanger at him as she spoke and was pleased to see the wariness in his eyes.

'However, all I'm going to do is hook the hook part through the zipper tab. Gives me more to hold on to when I heave it down.'

Mitch's skin went pale and for a moment she thought he might pass out again.

'Could you be a little less descriptive of your actions?' he said weakly.

She grinned at him.

'Don't worry,' she said. 'I'll be gentle with you.'

He groaned and closed his eyes, while Riley slipped the metal hook into the tab, then, using the wooden part as a handle, forced the zip back up.

'Now all I have to do is move the material that got caught out of the way before I pull it down again,' she said, and when he cringed, she added, 'We're not going to get up close and personal here. I assume you're wearing underpants.'

She hoped the strangled groaning noise he made was assent, but why he was getting so hot and bothered when she was the one doing all the work...

And suffering mammoth embarrassment, although she hoped to hell it didn't show. Acting cool, calm and collected was the only way to get through this embarrassing situation.

Coolly, she slipped the coathanger out of the way, then calmly she began to slide the zip back down.

Well, almost calmly. Her fingers were beginning to shake a little, and she could feel perspiration breaking out on her brow.

But it was when the zip stopped and she knew she'd have to slip her fingers inside his trousers to ease the problem out of the way that her cool finally deserted her, and all control over the blood that frequently swamped her cheeks was lost.

Face aflame with embarrassment, she fiddled and forced the little fold of zip material out of the way, finally getting the metal teeth past the bad spot and the opening fully undone.

A quick glance at Mitch's face showed him with his eyes

shut. She hoped he'd been that way throughout the proceedings.

'OK, you're all set now,' Riley said, heading for the door
just as fast as her feet would take her. Her face was cooling,
but at least with her back to him he wouldn't see the lin-
gering remnants of that fiery colour.

'Where are you going?' he asked, just as made it to the
door and was about to escape.

She turned back reluctantly to find him sitting up on the
bed, his left hand holding his trousers together at the waist.
With his right arm in the sling, his neck in a brace, he was
a pathetic specimen of manhood.

If you could class someone with such a great chest as a
pathetic specimen!

Disconcerted by her reaction to the chest, she hesitated,
then finally admitted, 'I don't know! I guess I could hang
around until Olivia gets back. Do you want me to phone
someone? Do you have family who'll help out?'

The look of panic in his brown eyes told her the answer,
and when he lifted his left hand she guessed he'd been
about to run it through his hair in an effort to make his
brain work better, but then he'd remembered his trousers
and dropped the hand back to retain his decency.

'My family's all in Melbourne, and even if they were
here, they're about as useful as busted eardrums,' he said,
then added bitterly, 'They pride themselves on being artis-
tic!'

Riley considered telling him he was lucky to have a family at all, but something in his voice told her he knew that—
he just knew he couldn't call on them for emergency relief!

'Friends?' she asked hopefully.

Mitch glanced at his watch.

'One's about to board a plane for the States—well, in a
couple of weeks, he's going—but his fiancée's going on
ahead and Peter's putting her on a plane today. You met

Brett at the hospital. His idea of helping would be to order pizzas for dinner and phone a few friends to come over to cheer me up. My partner Harry is much the same. Besides, if I'm out of action, he'll have to take the after-hours calls so he's out.'

A strange feeling of doom was creeping up on Riley.

'There must be someone!' she told him, and hoped he didn't hear the panic in her voice. 'What about your patients?'

He sent a scornful look zapping towards her.

'My patients are all pregnant women or nursing mothers who are actually quite involved in their own families at this stage of their lives.'

'Well, you make some suggestions!' she told him. 'After all, it's your problem, not mine.'

And with that she stalked out of the room, ignoring a whispered suggestion in her head that it might just possibly be her fault he'd been injured. After all, if he hadn't caught her when the ladder had tipped over, he wouldn't have suffered a dislocated shoulder and she could very well have ended up with two broken legs.

Olivia's arrival home put paid to further introspection. She was full of news of what she'd done, and blithely unconcerned about either her father's welfare or who was to take care of her in Mrs Rush's absence. After being told her father was in the bathroom, she turned on the television, fed a video into the machine and proceeded to dance to the tape she'd selected.

'I'd have kept her longer,' Clare, who'd been at school with Riley, said, 'but she's such an active child, she'd tired my lot out.'

She looked around the house as if expecting to see someone else.

'How's Mitch?' she asked. 'Is he still in hospital?'

'Mitch? Is that his name?'

Clare frowned.

'What do you call him?'

'Dr Hammond, of course,' Riley said, then light dawned. 'I don't know him,' she explained. 'Not personally. I've been here, working. He'd contracted Dennison's to build an extension, and Dad's hurt his back.'

Clare laughed.

'So, a few days back in town and it's Riley to the rescue. *And* back in the building trade. Aren't you worried you'll run into Jack?'

Riley shook her head in exasperation.

'Of course I'll run into Jack. I don't know why none of you believe he and I parted amicably. We're still good friends and always will be. It's just our paths went different ways.'

Clare raised her eyebrows in a manner that suggested she didn't, and never would, believe that story, but she accepted it and changed tack.

'Does Mitch know what you do? Why you're back in Port?'

Riley shook her head.

'And there's no need for you or anyone else to tell him. If he decides to rent those rooms to Peter's replacement, then I guess he'll find out soon enough. Though from what I've seen of him, I'm sure life would be a lot simpler if I found rooms somewhere else. Like in another state!'

'Having second thoughts about leaving the Big Smoke?'

'No way!' Riley told her, shaking her head to emphasise the point. 'When I've been breathing fresh air, jogging on the beach every morning and fishing at night in the river? I'm more surprised I stayed away so long. I'm just not certain I'd be happy working in close proximity to Dr Hammond.'

'Mitch! His name's Mitch!'

Clare smiled and, to Riley's surprise, she leaned forward and kissed her cheek.

'Good luck!' she said, then she gave a little wave, poked her head into the living room to say goodbye to Olivia and departed.

'Good luck?' Riley muttered to herself. 'Why on earth would I need good luck?'

'Ms Dennison!'

The bellow came from the end of the house beyond the small bedroom. If Riley remembered the layout properly, there was a second bathroom down that way.

She followed the noise and tapped on the door.

'What's wrong now?' she asked through the panels. 'Toe stuck in the outlet?'

There was a heavy moment of silence then, in such restrained notes she knew he must be clinging with difficulty to the last vestiges of his temper, he said, 'There are no towels in here.'

'I guess Mrs Rush took them out and washed them before she left,' Riley suggested.

'I do not give a damn what Mrs Rush did before she left.' The control was obviously slipping fast. 'I need a towel.'

Riley considered walking away. And possibly laughing loudly as she did so. Then realised if she'd had two broken legs she wouldn't have been walking anywhere, and she weakened.

'Provided you don't expect me to dry you, I'll get you one,' she said, and heard the faint echoes of his explosion of wrath as she hurried back to the living room.

'Where do you keep clean towels?' she asked Olivia.

The little girl looked blankly at her for a moment, no doubt her mind still on the dance steps she'd been doing, then she said, 'Towels?'

'Clean towels? For the bathroom? There must be a cupboard where Mrs Rush puts them after they've been washed.'

Light dawned in the blue eyes.

'They're in the towel cupboard,' she said, waving her hand towards the hall before turning her attention back to the TV screen.

Thinking harsh thoughts about spoilt children, Riley started searching, finding first the cupboard housing mops, brooms and the vacuum cleaner, then finally a linen closet.

'You took your time,' Mitch told her when she opened the bathroom door a mere four inches and thrust the towel and a bathmat inside. 'I've dried in the air and probably have pneumonia by now.'

'I should be so lucky!' Riley told him, then she stormed back down the hall. She'd lock the ladder into the small bedroom, and leave. Let him sort out his own life. It was none of her damn business.

'I'm hungry—what's for dinner?' Olivia asked as Riley relocked the small bedroom and pocketed the key.

'You'll have to ask your father,' Riley told her, hoping she sounded firmer than she felt.

But his accident had been partly her fault. Make that all her fault. If she hadn't missed the step on the ladder, he wouldn't have had to catch her, wouldn't have fallen, or hit his head.

Guilt forced her to add,   'What would you like for dinner? Shall we see what's in the refrigerator? Perhaps Mrs Rush had something there, ready to cook.'

'She was going to cook lamb chops,' Olivia told her, but she left the television and led the way towards the kitchen.

'Go back and turn off the TV and take out your video,' Riley told her. As Olivia stared at her in total bewilderment, Riley wondered if she'd ever been told to do anything.

'It's noisy,' Riley added. 'And if no one's watching it, it should be turned off.'

Olivia stood her ground.

'Mrs Rush never makes me turn it off.'

'Mrs Rush isn't here,' Riley pointed out. 'And I'm not *making* you do anything. I'm asking you, which is different. Now, please, Olivia, turn off the television.'

The blue eyes hardened, and the baby lips thinned into a mutinous line.

Riley turned away, pretending she hadn't seen the warning signs.

'I'm going to call the puppy I keep Penny. Have you thought of a name for yours?'

A scuffle of footsteps, then blessed silence, and Olivia was back within a minute.

'Mitch is a nice name,' she said.

Riley smiled at her.

'But who'd come when you called? The puppy or your dad?'

As Olivia considered this, and began to offer alternative names for a dog, Riley considered the contents of the refrigerator. Sure enough, six lamb chops were set out on a plate, covered with cling wrap to keep them fresh.

Cautiously, because it felt wrong to be investigating the contents of someone else's fridge, Riley opened the meat tray. More packs of lamb chops suggested Olivia's reply hadn't been a lucky guess.

'Do you have lamb chops every night?' she asked Olivia, who shook her head in denial.

'On Mondays and Tuesdays, that's when Mrs Rush has days off, we have fish and chips or pizza and sometimes Daddy takes me into town for McDonald's.'

'No wonder he needs a wife!' Riley murmured under her breath, shuddering at the dreariness of a diet of lamb chops five nights a week, with hamburgers, pizza or fish and chips the only regular variety.

But the mention of Mrs Rush's regular days off raised another issue.

'And who looks after you on Mrs Rush's days off?' Riley asked, pulling out the plate of lamb chops and setting them on the kitchen bench.

'Daddy does,' Olivia informed her. 'The pre-school bus drops me at his office and I talk to the fish in the fish tank until he's ready to go home. Harry does the night calls on those nights and some weekends and Daddy does the other nights.'

Riley nodded. She knew enough about the group to place Harry as Dr Harry Dobbs, the second O and G specialist. And to know he was neither married nor a local so would be unlikely to know anyone who could take Mrs Rush's place at short notice.

Dr Hammond was supposed to rest, and with his neck in a brace and his arm in a sling he was pretty useless anyway. So guess who'd be stuck with fixing their dinner?

Olivia, tiring of the name game, disappeared again, and the return of the dance music told Riley where she'd gone. Giving in to the inevitable, Riley tackled the meal preparations.

'You're still here?' the man whose bacon she was saving said ungraciously.

'Did you think Olivia was cooking your dinner?' Riley snapped at him. She'd peeled skin off her forefinger using a strange potato peeler, burnt her thumb on the grill when the handle on the grill pan collapsed, and on top of all that the smell of the meat cooking was making her feel extremely hungry.

'You didn't have to do it,' he protested, but the words didn't hold his usual forcefulness, and when she turned from the stove to look at him she saw weariness in his eyes and pain in the lines drawn down the side of his mouth.

The sight made something shift inside her chest. Hopefully, it was nothing more than sympathy for his plight. The simple pity she would have felt for any person who'd had more than his share of problems over such a short period of time.

She smiled at him.

'I thought it was the least I could do when I'd caused your injury by plummeting down into your arms,' she said, speaking lightly so he wouldn't make too much of it.

'But—' Mitch began, then stopped abruptly.

Boy! Had *she* ever given him an opening! He'd lain in the bath, desperately trying to work out what to do next. Once he was feeling better, he was sure he'd be able to get a temporary replacement for Mrs Rush, but right now, with his mind still hazy from either the fall or the anaesthetic, and his shoulder aching like hell...

'Well, I guess if you put it that way...' he said, and he raised his good hand to his forehead and tried a small swaying motion which Celeste would have admired for its dramatic appeal. Then he caught hold of the bench as if he needed its support to remain upright, and in a wavery voice added, 'A cold drink would be nice.'

For a moment he thought he might have gone too far, for the cool eyes narrowed and he could all but see the cogs turning in Riley's head. But she reached out to steady him, and held his arm while he slipped onto one of the stools at the bar which divided the kitchen from the informal family room.

'I'll see what's available in the cold drink department,' she said, a blandness in her voice masking any emotion.

As she swung open the door of the fridge, Mitch spotted a cold can of light ale. That's what a man needed at the end of a horrendous weekend!

'The beer will do,' he murmured, and she spun back towards him, the flash of satisfaction in her eyes telling him more clearly than words that he wasn't going to get it.

'Not on top of an anaesthetic,' she said. 'In fact, Brett was very definite about you not having any alcohol!'

'You make it sound as if I need to be kept away from the stuff,' Mitch complained. 'I'm not an alcoholic.'

Eyebrows rose above grey-green-blue eyes.

'Well, I'm not the person in this kitchen who had a hangover yesterday,' she sniped.

Which was when Mitch realised that keeping her here wasn't nearly such a good idea as it had at first appeared.

Although the drink she produced, soda with a tang of lemon, was so refreshing he almost forgave her.

Until he smelt the smoke.

'Something's on fire!'

She hurled herself towards the stove, and grabbed at the handle of the griller, yelped with pain and dropped the lot on the floor. The flames, perhaps affected by the downdraught, flickered and died. Mitch peered across the bench.

'Cooked or cremated?' he asked, delighted with this turn of events. Up until now it had been he making a total idiot of himself!

'It was your fault!' she said wrathfully, flinging the charred embers into the bin. 'Coming in and nearly fainting like that. If you'd stayed in your room—rested, like the doctor said—this would never have happened.'

'Something smells.' The smoke must have broken through the thrall holding Olivia to the television. 'Ooh, did you burn the dinner, Riley? Daddy doesn't like burnt dinner and nor do I.'

She climbed up on a stool beside her father and added, 'And could I have a drink like his, please?'

Mitch saw the look in Riley's eyes and guessed she was wondering which of them she'd strangle first, then, to his surprise, she smiled.

Not at him, of course, but at Olivia, but he still saw the smile and noticed how it made Riley's eyes seem bluer.

'I think you're old enough to get your own drink,' she told his daughter, and Mitch forgot about smiling eyes and waited for Olivia's reaction.

But before she could utter a protest, Riley was speaking again.

'I made your father's with soda water and a squeeze of lemon, but it might taste sour to you. There's some lemonade in the refrigerator. If I got it out and found you a glass, could you pour it yourself?'

To Mitch's amazement, the tyrant who had ruled his house for the last few years slid off the stool and trotted into the kitchen, a smile that suggested this was a rare treat lighting her beautiful face.

He glanced at Riley, wondering if perhaps she had some miraculous powers, but there was nothing visible, no angel wings sprouting from her back. And when he tried a mental halo on top of that riot of dark red-brown curls he had to chuckle. Boy! Would she cause some trouble in heaven!

'I hope you're not laughing at me,' the non-angel threatened. She'd set a bottle of lemonade and a plastic beaker on a chair for Olivia, and was now holding an open carton of eggs in her hand, apparently examining the contents.

Certain of the devastation she could wreak, he assured her it wasn't the case.

She must have been satisfied, for she proceeded to ignore him, addressing her next remark to Olivia.

'Do you like eggs, sweetie?'

Olivia, concentrating fiercely on the operation of getting lemonade into the beaker, nodded briefly.

'Then I'll make a frittata and you can have that instead of the chops. I reckon you could both do with a little variety in your diet.'

Satisfied Olivia was finished, she retrieved the lemonade, then lifted the beaker and put it on the bench in front of

Olivia's stool, motioning to his daughter to resume her perch.

'What about me?' Mitch demanded, as the woman then turned away and began to hunt through the cupboards, presumably for whatever dishes she required. 'Aren't you going to ask my food preferences?'

'You're an adult, and unless eggs bring you out in hives you'll eat frittata, and like it.'

She paused, tossing her head just enough to set the curls dancing.

'Or there are always the burnt chops. I could retrieve a couple from the bin.'

Mitch gave up, though not without giving her what he hoped was a very dirty look!

Within minutes whatever she was doing with the eggs and other ingredients she'd been digging out of the cupboards began to smell very appetising. He began to hope she'd missed the dirty look.

Riley told herself this was the same as whipping up something for her father's dinner, but her father sitting at the breakfast bar, watching her potter in the kitchen, had never made her nerves feel tight or her skin so super-sensitive.

Mitch Hammond is a man who, for all his feeble protests yesterday, is obviously still carrying a torch for his first wife, she reminded herself. Not only is the woman the mother of his child, but she's so voluptuously beautiful she'd barely been in Hollywood a month before she'd been dubbed the brightest new star—and the Sex Goddess.

Five-ten and skinny, with a fairly ordinary face and too much red hair couldn't really compete! So, whatever it was that was tightening her nerves and sensitising her skin had better stop right now. With this job to supervise for her father, and decisions to be made about her future, she couldn't afford any distractions.

Particularly when she was cooking. She peered at the egg mix she had in the frying pan and, satisfied it was almost set, lifted it off the hotplate, sprinkled grated cheese over the top and put it under the grill to brown.

While that was happening, she mashed the potatoes and threw together some salad ingredients, found a variety of dressings in the pantry and pulled them out.

'Do you eat here at the breakfast bar?' she asked, finding the cutlery drawer first go and selecting one large and one small knife and one large and one small fork. Added a teaspoon to the mix in case Olivia wasn't up to forks.

'When Mrs Rush isn't here,' Olivia told her.

Reassured she had it right, Riley set the cutlery down in front of the Hammond father and daughter. She grabbed a pot-holder before rescuing the frittata, so beautifully browned and smelling so tempting she had to swallow down on her own hunger.

Setting the pan down on a board, she cut the flat omelette into wedges, found two plates and slid a small wedge onto Olivia's and two wedges onto the doctor's.

'Aren't you having some?' Olivia asked.

Wrong person asking, Riley thought, and she shook her head.

'I've got to go home,' she replied. 'I'll have my dinner there.'

To her surprise Olivia's eyes filled with tears, but she didn't bellow, merely looked desperately unhappy.

'But who's going to look after me and Daddy?' she whispered, and Riley cursed herself for not thinking further than her own problems. Of course the little one was upset. First she'd seen her father carted off in an ambulance, then she'd returned home to find him with a neck brace and sling.

Riley forgot about serving their dinners and went around to give Olivia a hug.

'Your daddy's not badly hurt,' she said gently. 'The doc-

tor wants him to keep his neck still—that's why he put on
the special collar—and he has to rest his arm, but it's not
broken. He can still use it.'

Over Olivia's head, she sent eye messages to Mitch.
Come on, it's your turn to reassure her, she was trying to
tell him.

Talk about obtuse! He looked blankly back at her and
said nothing. In fact, when he moved his arm a fraction he
had the hide to groan. Just a little! Like a man desperately
trying to be brave about severe pain.

She'd give him pain!

Though not in front of his daughter.

Leaving Olivia, she finished serving their meals and this
time it was the father who protested.

'There's plenty there—please, join us. You're doing us
a huge favour, staying on like this.'

The words were polite enough but the gleam in his eyes
challenged her to argue, reminding her with one look that
it was her fault he was injured.

Talk about rubbing it in.

But eating with them seemed too cosy somehow. Not a
good idea, given her tight nerves.

'I can't stay, I've got to feed my animals,' she explained
to Olivia, not the father, and although Olivia pouted, it was
the father who replied.

'We could all go over to your place and do that after
dinner. Olivia would like to see the puppies, and you could
pack a bag while you're there.'

Olivia began to bounce up and down on her stool with
delight, but no amount of bouncing delight was going to
have Riley fall for this ploy.

'Pack a bag?' she demanded. 'I agreed to help out with
your meal, not take Mrs Rush's place for ever. All you
need is rest. A good night's sleep and you'll be fit as a

fiddle in the morning. And you can dial an employment agency with your left hand, so what's the problem?'

'Couldn't you stay the night?' Olivia begged. 'It would be such fun. And in the morning you'll be right here, ready to do your job. You won't even have to drive.'

She sounded so hopeful, as if having someone to stay the night was the ultimate in treats. Riley felt the beginning of the guilt she knew would grow enormously when she disappointed the child. She closed her eyes and prayed for inspiration.

Nothing came. Well, nothing startling.

'The men won't be working here tomorrow, Olivia,' she explained. 'I've organised for the exterminator, Dave's owner, to come and bring Dave so they can find any more termites.'

'Oh, is Dave coming? Could I stay home and watch? He likes me, he really does.'

This time she imbued the idea of watching a dog sniff termites with such extraordinary delight that Riley was glad it was her father who'd have to make that decision.

'If Riley's here to keep an eye on you, you can stay home,' the wretch said, and Riley knew he was deliberately trapping her into caring for his child.

'Although I won't be seeing patients all wrapped up like this, I won't be able to stay at home all day. I'll have to organise for my patients to see Harry, and I have to talk to the other people in the building about a personnel matter and catch up on some paperwork.'

From the way he spoke, Riley guessed he often talked about his work to Olivia, not talking down to her but telling her what was going on. That earned him a tick of approval!

The first so far!

But now two pairs of eyes, one brown, and one blue, were focussed on her—awaiting a decision.

Though not for long. Mitch Hammond must have seen her weakening. He nodded to the remainder of the frittata.

'Your dinner's getting cold.'

CHAPTER FIVE

FOUR hours later, Riley lay in the strange bed and wondered just where her guilt at being responsible for Mitch's injury would eventually lead. True to his word, he and Olivia had accompanied her to her father's home, where a well-fed mother and eight sleepy pups had made a lie of her earlier excuse.

Olivia had picked out the dog she wanted.

'At least I had the presence of mind to tell her it was too young to leave its mother,' Riley muttered to herself, 'or I'd be dog-sitting as well as child-minding and doctor-watching.'

Was there such an occupation?

She thought of the way his streaky blond hair curled slightly behind his ears, and the way his eyes seemed to narrow when he was trying not to smile. Might not be a bad job, she decided sleepily as she drifted off to sleep.

To be woken, what seemed only minutes later, by a small body bouncing on the bed.

'Do you bounce on Mrs Rush like this?' she demanded, as the tousle-haired child put her arms around her shoulders and pressed a wet kiss on her cheek.

'Mrs Rush is the housekeeper,' the four-going-on-forty-year-old replied. 'You're my friend and soon you're going to give me a dog, but first you'd better get up because I'm hungry.'

Riley pulled her left arm out from under the covers and squinted at her watch.

'It's only six o'clock,' she complained.

Olivia favoured her with a beaming smile.

'That's what Daddy said when I told him I was hungry. Then he said to try you, because builders have to get up early.'

Pity I didn't fall harder, Riley thought with grim regret. I might have killed him.

'I'm not always a builder,' she told Olivia. 'Just helping out my dad for a few days.'

Disappointment clouded the bright eyes.

'So you won't get out of bed?'

Riley had steeled herself against the clouded eyes, but the quivering lip was her undoing.

'Of course I'll get up, little one,' she said, returning the hug and planting a kiss of her own on the so-soft cheek. 'Why don't you go on ahead and get out whatever cereal you have for breakfast, and I'll come in to help you in a few minutes.'

She used the bathroom first, cleaning her teeth and splashing water on her face. As she emerged, feeling slightly more human, Mitch was standing outside the door.

'Someone ripped half the tiles off the wall in mine so I have to share,' he reminded her, and Riley, who'd at first been mesmerised by the darkly shadowed jawline of the unshaven man, regained enough composure to scowl at him.

'Builders aren't allowed to start work on jobs until seven,' she informed him. 'Which means we do not have to get up all that early!'

He was totally unabashed. In fact, he had the hide to grin at her.

'Wake you, did she? She targeted me first and I really thought, with what was a medically ordered day off, I might be able to go back to sleep.'

He held his arms wide, as if to show off a body already visible enough to Riley, then winced as the movement hurt his injured shoulder.

'It didn't work and here I am.' He paused, peering at her, and she felt his scrutiny like a feather brushing across her skin. 'And injured though I am,' he added, getting his reminder in, 'I can manage to pour cereal into a bowl and add milk. You can go back to bed if you want to.'

Riley contented herself with another scowl, and a reminder to put on the neck collar, and use the sling to rest his shoulder, then she ducked past him and hurried back into Mrs Rush's bedroom. With the door shut behind her, she studied her reflection in the mirror.

Did she look tired and haggard that he'd suggested she go back to bed? She hadn't slept *that* badly!

She pulled on her overalls, bundled her hair under a scarf then, with slow, reluctant steps, walked towards the kitchen.

Olivia had apparently finished her breakfast and the television was on at full volume yet again. Was it her sole form of entertainment?

Didn't anyone care enough to find more useful things for her to do?

She confronted the 'anyone' whose place it was to care, but didn't feel she could bring up that particular subject.

'Dad has switched his men to another job,' she told him—should she continue to call him Dr Hammond? Or change to Mitch? He hadn't suggested it. 'Once we know where the termites are, and where they've been, I'll know if we need engineering advice or can simply replace the unsafe timber.'

He did his shuddering thing again, and waved his hand as if to dismiss any responsibility.

'Do whatever you think is best,' he told her. 'Just get it sorted out.'

Then he frowned.

'Will you be here all day? Would you mind keeping an

eye on Olivia? She can go to her pre-school otherwise, but her heart's set on staying home to see the dog at work.'

He seemed almost embarrassed and Riley guessed he didn't ask for favours often.

Perhaps he didn't like to feel obligated.

'I'll pay you for it, of course,' he added, confirming the guess and making her feel acutely uncomfortable.

'Oh, no!' she said, looking at the sling and neck brace. 'It's the least I can do.'

An expression she couldn't read briefly shadowed his face. Almost like guilt, but that was unlikely. More embarrassment perhaps?

'Well, I should have someone to replace Mrs Rush by this evening,' he added, then he smiled and Riley's reaction was so instantaneous she had to turn away in case he saw it.

Nerves tightening, skin leaping to full alertness, heat spreading where it seldom spread these days.

Damn!

And double damn, because she wasn't nearly as certain as he was that he'd have a replacement for Mrs Rush by this evening. Unless the town had changed more than she realised in the years she'd been away.

Mitch folded the paper he'd been pretending to read while he'd waited for his temporary housekeeper to appear in the kitchen.

Though he had no idea why her presence in his house should be proving so distracting. He barely knew the woman with the straight slim back and long, pale neck who was fussing over his kitchen sink!

But he'd known plenty who were better-looking.

So why did he want her to turn around?

Get out of here, mate, he told himself.

Now!

He flopped the paper on the bench.

'I'm going in to the office—I can handle the car easily enough. I'll contact an employment agency from there.'

That spun her around!

'Make sure you get references and check them out because sometimes people lie, and you'll have to interview the people the agency suggests yourself, not just trust their word.'

He was surprised by her vehemence, but what she said made sense. Although his hope of having someone installed by this evening was fading fast.

'I could stay another night if you can't get someone to start immediately,' Riley offered, although the way she spoke made it obvious that being hung, drawn and quartered would have been an equally attractive option.

'Thank you,' he said, pretending he hadn't heard the reservations in her voice.

Actually, with Riley Dennison still consumed by guilt, keeping her here shouldn't prove too difficult. Which reduced the urgency in replacing Mrs Rush. He'd get Clare to handle it. She could even do the interviews. After all, she was a mother. She'd know just what he needed.

'No!'

'No?' Mitch echoed the word and stared in total disbelief at his secretary. She'd told him off from time to time, but had never ever said no to him before. 'What do you mean no?'

'I mean no I won't do the interviews for you to choose a temporary housekeeper. I'm not entirely stupid, Mitch,' she said. 'I know exactly what will happen. I pick one out for you and every time she loses a sock or doesn't iron your collar properly, or does anything else to upset you you'll blame me.'

'But why should she do anything to upset me?' Mitch demanded.

Clare had the gall to smile at him.

'Ask the question another way. Why should you get upset over trivial things that happen in your life? Because you're not happy, that's why. You're not leading a normal life for a man your age. You don't go out, won't date women, you have no social life at all. You're like a monk who didn't choose the life and you're angry and resentful because you feel it was thrust on you. Which it wasn't. Celeste left, that's all. She didn't kill you, or castrate you, or leave you locked in a strait-jacket.'

Mitch listened with growing anger to his secretary's tirade, and when she paused for breath he asked, 'How long have you been working all this out? And is it just you, or does the entire building agree with this version of my life?'

He stopped long enough to glare at her, then added, 'Which is wrong!'

'Oh, yeah?' she said, and again had the hide to smile. 'When did you last have sex?'

And with that she whirled out of the room, poking her head back in long enough to say, 'I'll phone the employment agency and handle the appointments for the interviews. After that, it's up to you.'

Thrust into a monastic life, was he?

It was none of her business when he'd last had sex.

When Celeste had left for the States, they'd both assumed she'd be coming back. Doing the one picture in which she had a part, then returning. They'd even talked about a possible family relocation, should her career take off, but it had seemed so unlikely, the talks hadn't been serious.

Unlikely?

That was the first laugh.

Once the Sex Goddess thing began, and she realised the title was hardly apt for a married woman with a small child, she'd soon dispelled any idea of all of them moving to L.A.

And the fact that she could make that decision so easily was the second laugh!

But it had still been two years before he'd accepted she wasn't ever coming back. Two years when his main priority had been trying to make up for her loss to Olivia, and when, personally, he'd been so confused, dating, sex and a social life had been the last things on his mind.

This year had been slightly better, but there'd been the divorce to negotiate and habits had already taken hold. Probably because he kept saying no, people had stopped inviting him places—or introducing him to available women.

Now he came to think about it, he couldn't remember when he'd last had sex!

The image of a tall, slim woman in overalls came to mind, and he frowned. Harry, knocking then entering without an invitation, said, 'You shouldn't be here, Mitch. You're obviously in pain.'

'I am not in pain, and I'd appreciate it if the people in this practice would stop making assumptions about me, my health or my life in general.'

'Clare been telling you off?' his partner said sympathetically. 'Women can be hell, can't they?'

He hitched his hip on the far side of Mitch's desk.

'How's your patient load today? Anyone who can't be put off until later in the week? I could take an extra five without too much hassle.'

'I haven't checked,' Mitch told him. 'But five would certainly pull it up. In fact, I wouldn't be surprised if I only had late morning patients. I'm so far behind in paperwork I've been asking Clare to keep Monday's appointments as light as possible.'

'And what's happening about Peter's replacement? Only another fortnight until he goes. Will whoever it is keep the rooms?'

Mitch sighed.

'Yesterday, I'd decided, yes, definitely. I'd just sign the person up, but today I've started wondering again. There's enough tension in the building with Hugh and Frances at odds. The whole idea of working as a team is to give our patients and their families a complete and convenient service. But to do that, at least the majority of the professionals should get along.'

'Well, I don't care either way,' Harry replied. 'Although Peter worked out really well. And having him in the same building made appointments easier for a lot of families. Go ahead and sign the lease with the replacement then tell everyone that's what's happening.'

Mitch was tempted, but before he could voice further doubts about the outcome of such autocratic behaviour Harry was speaking again.

'If you're going to play nice and ask for opinions, you'll get a no from Tracey, who wants the rooms, and I wish you the best of luck in trying to get an agreement from Frances and Hugh. Were they always like this? Always at each other's throats? Jenny thinks they're in love but refuse to admit it.'

The idea that the two antagonistic paediatricians could possibly be in love was so ludicrous that Mitch laughed. Hugh was a born bachelor. Never without a lovely lady escort but with marriage further from his mind than Mars.

While as for Frances, her insistence on being called by her full name typified her slightly strait-laced approach to life. In fact, Mitch suspected her disapproval of Hugh's private life had a lot to do with her antagonistic attitude towards her colleague.

'Surely not!' Mitch protested.

'Stranger things have happened,' Harry reminded him, then turned the conversation back to work, asking, 'If you're going to do the consensus thing, won't you have to introduce the replacement to everyone before asking for their final decision? It's pointless putting it to them otherwise.'

Mitch tried to remember what Peter had said about his replacement. Someone who'd worked at Sydney's new children's hospital with him. Easygoing. Excellent professional.

Had he mentioned when this paragon was arriving in the town?

'I guess I'll have to get him in here for everyone to meet before signing anything,' Mitch agreed. 'Though Peter certainly rapped the guy.'

Harry laughed. 'For all the good it did!' he told his friend. 'The guy's a girl—well, a woman, I guess you'd call her. Close to thirty. I read the copy of her CV which Clare passed around. She's had experience in all the fields Peter had, but has also done some counselling work with pregnant teenagers as well, which would be an added bonus for you and me.'

Mitch nodded. Now that he thought about it, he'd also read the CV, or had glanced at it before handing it to Clare and asking her to circulate it. Wasn't it a Susan someone?

'Well, I'd vote to have her on the premises,' Harry added. 'For a start, it'll be less disruptive for Peter's patients. They might be meeting a new face but the surroundings will be familiar.'

'You're right. But I'll get her in to meet everyone before signing anything.'

Then, as something else occurred to him, he frowned.

'Talking about patient disruption, when is she actually starting? I know Peter said she'd be working with him for a while before he went. Is it today she's beginning, or next week?'

'Next week,' Harry told him. 'She's been working in Sydney but she's been commuting up and back the last few weekends to meet as many of Peter's patients as possible. Then she'll have that final week with him in the rooms.'

Mitch gave the unknown woman a tick for dedication, then frowned, wondering why Peter hadn't seen fit to introduce her on one of the flying visits.

'Apparently her father's not well,' Harry added, unknowingly answering Mitch's thoughts. 'That's the main reason she wanted to come back to Port.'

Having delivered this final bit of information, Harry straightened up and seemed about to leave, then hesitated, studying his colleague for a moment.

'You look terrible. Should you be here?'

Mitch grimaced at him.

'Here is better than my place,' he admitted. 'I've an exterminator there with a dog, sniffing out termites, a manic builder ripping holes in my walls and telling me the building may be structurally unsound, Mrs Rush has taken off to cluck over her daughters' triplets so I've no housekeeper, and Clare refuses to organise a replacement. Says it's my job!'

Harry made sympathetic noises, but Mitch could see the smile lurking in his eyes.

'Don't you laugh!' he warned. 'It wouldn't be the first time in the last few days murder has crossed my mind.'

Harry did laugh then, but sobered soon after.

'Who'll be looking after Olivia until you find someone? Jenny would have taken her, but she's just got a new commission and is working all hours of the day and night, getting the work for the exhibition finished before she starts on it.'

Mitch nodded his thanks. Harry's girlfriend got on well with Olivia, but she was an artist preparing for a major showing opening within weeks at a local gallery. With a commission on top of that...

'At the moment I'm blackmailing the builder into caring

for her,' he explained, 'but how long that will last, I don't know.'

Harry looked puzzled, but as the phone rang at that moment Mitch didn't have time to explain.

Which was just as well as he wasn't at all certain he wanted anyone to know his 'builder' was a woman. And a young one at that.

'Yes, Mrs Lynch,' he said as Clare put the caller through. 'How can I help you today?'

Mrs Lynch described the sharp pain she was experiencing in the right side of her abdomen, while Mitch brought her details up on the computer screen.

Six months into her first pregnancy, and everything going smoothly.

'You've got a couple of bands of muscle that start up on your ribs and cross down to your pelvis. They keep your tummy tucked in when you're not pregnant and actually help digestion as well. The external oblique muscle is a broad band of muscle fibre and the internal oblique a smaller muscle.'

He paused while Mrs Lynch repeated the names.

'These have to stretch during pregnancy and the internal in particular is inclined to cramp. I'd say that's what your pains are, but I'll put you through to Clare and she'll see when she can fit you in. Do you mind seeing Dr Dobbs? I'm only here doing some paperwork and he's seeing my patients for a couple of days.'

'Oh, no,' Mrs Lynch assured him. 'I like seeing Dr Dobbs now and then. He's so sexy! Though I do hope you're on duty when the baby comes. Sexy isn't everything, is it?'

Mitch frowned at the receiver as he put her through to Clare.

Sexy isn't everything, indeed!

Did the woman think he was asexual?

What a put-down.

He pulled the tray of paperwork Clare had dumped on his desk closer and lifted the first item, a twenty page statistical form to be completed for the government. Clare had pencilled in most of the answers, but there were enough blanks to give him heartburn just looking at them.

He set it aside and lifted the next sheaf.

Ha! Much better. Patient reports to referring doctors. His computer program almost wrote these itself. He'd tackle that job first.

But his satisfaction didn't last long. The second referral was from the free clinic staffed by off-duty doctors, and the patient, Blythe Reid, was a sixteen-year-old who was currently living in a small seedy caravan with two girl friends.

Peter's suggestion of having someone with experience in teenage pregnancy counselling within the building suddenly seemed extremely sensible. Important enough, in fact, for Mitch to leave the letter and call Clare.

'See when's the earliest you can get all the tenants together for a meeting. Don't bother Peter with it—I know he's flat out—but I'd like the therapists there as well. If we can't get the lot today, I'll make do with whoever *can* come.'

'To talk about renting Peter's rooms?' Clare asked.

'Of course,' Mitch said crisply, then he hung up before she told him the decision should have been made when Peter had first announced his departure, not now, a fortnight before he left.

Mitch ran his fingers through his hair and felt its length. Getting a haircut was another thing he should have done.

Then he thought of other—different coloured—hair and groaned.

How long *had* it been since he'd had sex?

*   *   *

'I don't see why we had to have a meeting,' Tracey, the occupational therapist, said when the meeting Mitch had called to order only minutes earlier had erupted into chaos. 'You own the building and you can lease the rooms to whomever you please, so if you think we really need a psychologist within the group, it's up to you to decide, then you just tell us.'

The way she spoke told him how she felt about the 'need'!

Jill, the physio, was frowning at him so he nodded towards her, to let her have her say.

'Tracey's right, it's up to you. I don't know what's wrong with you these days, Mitch. You used to be such a decisive man!'

Mitch glanced at Clare who was present to take the minutes of the meeting, but she didn't look as if she was thinking it was lack of sex causing his problem.

'There's nothing wrong with me. I'm just trying to get a consensus,' he told Jill.

'You'll never please everyone,' she retorted. 'And it's not as if we'll be employing this person. We all work independently, although we share a building and pass referrals to each other. Personally, I think Peter did an excellent job and added an extra dimension to the group dynamics. I can't see any reason why the person taking over his patients can't also take over the rooms.'

'Not without interviewing him!' Frances said, obviously appalled by such a glib decision. 'He might not get on with us.'

'It's not a him, it's a her,' Hugh reminded them. 'And if it's the her I saw chatting to Peter downtown last weekend, then I vote we forget the getting-to-know-you meeting and invite her to move right in.'

Naturally, Frances had to bite at the lure Hugh had dangled in front of her, and argument erupted again.

'Oh, for heaven's sake, you two. Get over it!' Mitch snapped.

The noise ceased immediately and five startled group members stared at their landlord and director of their loosely formed team, mouths agape as varying degrees of disbelief and astonishment held them in thrall.

'Clare, ask the woman to come in and meet us all as soon as possible. If Frances doesn't find anything offensive about her habits, she can sign the lease!'

And on that note he pushed back his chair and walked out of the room, taking care not to slam the door.

'There's nothing about career counselling for young teenagers in her CV,' he heard Frances say, and shook his head. He might have made a decision, but the argument was still raging.

And would continue—various parties following him into his office to voice their approval or disapproval.

Maybe he'd make a second decision and get a haircut. Then go home and—

Find out how bad the termite problem was?

Mitch groaned and held his head in his hands for a while to see if that would improve things, but when it didn't he turned resolutely back to the wire basket and tackled paperwork until the persistent ache in his shoulder suggested he'd used it enough for one morning.

He stood up and took the sheaf of completed work through to Clare, certain she'd be pleased with him for catching up.

'Susan Barker can come in at four-thirty on Friday,' she told him, but her eyes remained focussed on her computer screen. 'I've told the others, and if they want to meet her they can juggle their appointments to make the time.'

'I assume I'm free,' Mitch replied, wondering just what was holding his secretary's attention.

'Providing no one decides to have a baby,' Clare said,

though once again she didn't turn to face him. Could it be some form of avoidance tactic?

But why?

Perhaps she felt she'd overstepped an invisible boundary, asking him when he'd last had sex. But Clare had told him things for his own good before, and not gone into remote mode afterwards.

He was still puzzling over it a little later as he settled into the barber's chair, took off the protective collar and closed his eyes to make it easier to replay this morning's conversation. The barber murmured something about the weather, about an appeal—there was always an appeal for something going on—and continued with the usual patter of the haircut ritual.

It was the buzz of a shaver which finally alerted Mitch to disaster, and he opened his eyes and gazed in horror at the newly mown stripe, two inches wide, running down the centre of his scalp.

'What are you doing?' he bellowed at the man, struggling to get out of the enveloping cape so he could—

Do *something* physical to the idiot.

'I thought you wanted the head shave, sir,' the man, who was cowering back against his sink, said feebly. 'I asked and you said yes. It's free, you see. It's on the sign outside. I do it for free and you make a donation to the Leukemia Appeal. You can donate more than the haircut costs, of course, and most people get their friends to sponsor them. Like friends betting they would or wouldn't do it, see? I can't take it right off all at once, so I just trim it short, then shave it.'

Mitch slumped back down into the chair and stared at the reflection of this latest disaster.

His roof was about to come off, termites were eating through his walls, he had to wear a collar around his neck that made him look like an something from an ancient tribe of neck-stretchers, and now he had a stripe of too-short hair down the centre of his head.

'You being a doctor and all, I thought...' the man added lamely.

Mitch nodded to show he'd cooled off. He knew about the 'shave your head for cancer' idea, but had never considered joining the ever-increasing number of newly bald men in the town. For one thing, his patients might not like it.

'It's amazing how the women seem to go for the look,' the barber told him, growing bold enough to approach the chair once again. 'More often than not it's the wives and girlfriends as talk their men into it.'

He picked up his razor and held it in his hand, apparently waiting for some signal to continue.

'Well, you can't leave me like this,' Mitch told him. 'Cut the rest to match what you've done, but no shaving, understand. I refuse to go bald this early in my life, no matter what the cause.'

He watched, half repelled and half fascinated, as his hair fell to the ground, revealing a not badly shaped skull beneath the close crop.

'Not that I have a wife or girlfriend to admire any haircut!' he muttered gloomily, startling the barber so much he missed a bit.

But in the end the stranger looking back at him from the mirror was so unfamiliar he knew he'd have to buy a hat before he ventured too far from the shop. Or frighten himself every time he saw his new reflection in a shop window.

'I do sell caps.' The barber must have read his mind. 'Baseball caps—the kind the kids all wear. The money from the sales goes to the same appeal. You want one?'

Mitch nodded, and once the job was completed refitted his collar, then slapped the cap gratefully on his head.

Adding a large donation for the appeal, he finally left the shop, lighter in the pocket as well as in the head.

He drove home, certain things couldn't get worse, but the mere sight of Riley Dennison's truck dispelled that idea. She was like a harbinger of doom and wherever she was, things would almost certainly deteriorate.

This gloomy prediction was confirmed as he entered the house. The kitchen looked as if a bomb had hit it, and the frenzied barking of Dave the sniffer dog from the direction of his bedroom suggested there was worse to come.

'They're confined mainly to that back wall,' the muscle-bound exterminator told him cheerfully, when Mitch, failing to find either Riley or Olivia, caught up with him.

'You mean they're in the rafters right through from there to the small bedroom?' Mitch said faintly, picturing the roof crashing down on him as he slept.

Michael laughed with an aggravating heartiness.

'No, mate, you've no worries up there. They've been and gone, but not above this main bedroom. I'd say, back when-ever, they started on the side wall, where the small bedroom is, and got into the rafter that way, then maybe a previous owner had the place sprayed and got rid of them. Trouble was, he didn't replace the damaged timber, but Riley will see to that.'

Mitch was so relieved he didn't argue about who would see to it.

'You're saying the roof is sound, apart from that one rafter? Isn't that a bit of a coincidence?'

The huge shoulders lifted and dropped in a muscle-twitching shrug.

'No! Termites are funny things. Could be that particular timber tasted good to them, while the others didn't. Some timber they can't abide. Others are like chocolate to a chocoholic. Hard to keep 'em out.'

'Apparently the timber in the walls are the chocolate type,' Mitch said, pointing to the devastation in the kitchen.

'Oh, it's not so bad,' Michael assured him. 'Looks worse because Riley took all the gear out of the cupboards so she could get in to replace a couple of boards.'

He paused, looking directly at Mitch.

'I assume you do want Dennison's doing the job?'

Mitch didn't, but he could give no good reason for not letting Riley do it, and getting someone else would be time-consuming and probably frustrating.

'I suppose so,' he said grudgingly.

But if Michael was bothered by the lack of enthusiasm he didn't show it, merely nodding and calling to Dave, who'd discovered some leftover food scrap under a lounge chair.

'You got a fax at your office? I'll fax you through a quote tonight. You'd be best moving out when we do it, as I'll have to drill holes through the floor in places to get poison down into the ground.'

Drill holes in the floor?

As the words hit Mitch's consciousness, he lifted his cap to run his hand through his hair, then remembered he didn't have enough hair to run fingers through and clamped it back onto his head.

'Don't worry about a quote, just do it,' he muttered, then moved away so he couldn't hear the man telling him he should be more businesslike and compare prices before settling on a tradesman.

In the kitchen, he hunted through the chaos—which apparently was only the contents of a couple of cupboards—for a jar of instant coffee. Perhaps if he had a hot drink, and something to eat, he'd feel a whole lot better.

And if he remembered rightly, one of the cable TV channels had replays of the weekend football games. What with one thing and another, he hadn't even heard the results.

He made a sandwich, poured boiling water onto the instant coffee, set the mug and plate on a tray so he could carry it one-handed, then, feeling more at ease than he had for days, he carried the tray across to his favourite armchair. He flicked the remote towards the screen, turned on the power, wended his way through the channels to see what else was showing then, when he found the sports channel, he settled back with a contented sigh.

'Daddy, Daddy. Riley says we can go and stay at her place, with the dogs and puppies and Mr Riley's parrots and she's got a cat as well.'

Mitch sat up so quickly he slopped coffee down the pristine white business shirt he'd put on to go to work. He dumped the cup on the table and stared in horror at his daughter.

'I don't do laundry,' another voice said, and he turned his attention to the woman who'd walked into the room behind his daughter and was eyeing his stained shirt with obvious disgust.

CHAPTER SIX

'NO ONE asked you to do laundry!' Mitch snapped. 'Nor is there any necessity for us to stay with you. We're staying here.'

'While Michael drills holes through your floors and injects toxic chemicals into the ground?' Riley shrugged. 'Suit yourself, but I'd call it gross negligence to subject a young child to even the slightest risk that the fumes could harm her.'

She turned, heading towards the door. She'd done enough for this family. Let him fend for himself. Make his own decisions. He was a grown man after all.

He caught her as she reached the front porch. Grabbed her arm and spun her around.

'Wait!' he said, and she read the depths of his uncertainty in the dark eyes. 'I only meant I didn't want to put you out. None of this is your fault, so why should you have to put us up?'

His hand still held her arm, not tightly but with enough contact to send a warmth she couldn't remember feeling before coursing through her body. She studied his face, or what she could see of it beneath the brim of the baseball cap. A strong, straight nose drew her gaze to his mouth, to lips that were full, but not too full, well defined and, from the faint lines running down each side, much given to smiling.

A good-looking man, but not drop-dead handsome.

'Hotel somewhere.'

Which was when she realised he'd been talking, while

her thoughts had moved lower, to consider a firm, strong chin with the slightest of indentations.

Hotels! That's what they were discussing. Not chins, or lips…

'I tried the larger resort hotels for you because they have child-care facilities, but with the school holidays they're all booked out.'

The uncertainty in his eyes shifted to a kind of desperation.

'And there are no flats, no cabins at the caravan park, no motel rooms. Which is why I thought of my place. Well, my father's place, actually. I'm living with him. It's only for a few days while Michael works here and until the fumes clear. A safety precaution. My father's happy to look after Olivia when she gets home from her pre-school. He doesn't take kindly to doctor's orders to rest and is bored to death. He'll enjoy it.'

Mitch dropped her arm and stepped back.

'I can't expect your father to take care of my daughter.' He spoke firmly, then looked directly at her and smiled.

A much-used smile, as Riley had guessed. One that came to the fore when he wanted something. She waited for the punchline.

'But she obviously likes you and as you can't be working on the house while the exterminators are here, could you—would you—be willing to take care of her? I can still drop her at pre-school and arrange for the bus to take her back to your place, so it wouldn't be a full-time commitment, and I can collect her there when I finish work…'

Riley watched the play of emotions on his face as the full implications of being without his housekeeper dawned.

'If I find accommodation—' he began.

'If?' she said. 'Don't you ever listen? There *is* no accommodation.'

Then, feeling sorry for him—and some responsibility for at least part of his plight—she weakened.

'I'll mind Olivia when I'm there,' she promised, while her conscience told her this was the time to tell him she would be starting work next week.

Hopefully in his building!

As his tenant.

But given the way he obviously felt about her—blaming her for all his misfortunes—if she mentioned the job he might cancel Friday's appointment and rent his rooms to someone else.

And though she'd find other rooms, it would be a hassle, both for her and for the patients.

'I still don't see why your father should be put out,' Mitch grumbled, but Olivia, who'd disappeared after the initial announcement, returned, dragging an overnight bag behind her.

'I've packed my things,' she announced. 'Can we go?'

This time Riley watched the man battle against his determination to avoid accepting her help. She saw him lift his left hand and guessed he'd run it through his hair—a habit when he was thinking.

His fingers came in contact with the cap and dislodged it slightly, revealing short-trimmed hair.

'Let's see it!' Riley said, and reached out to whip off his cap.

But it wasn't the haircut that attracted her attention, it was the look in his eyes as she moved closer.

A look that sent a shiver of presentiment rippling through her body.

Spending any more time with this man, who was now squatting down so Olivia could run her hands over his head and study this new and very trendy-looking father, was a big mistake.

As for working in the same building as him…

Although that would be different. She'd see more of the paediatricians than the O and G men and there were professional behaviour standards behind which she could hide.

But...

'Go and pack, Daddy, so we can get to Riley's place in time to feed the birds.'

Riley waited for Mitch's reaction. She guessed he'd rather sleep on the beach than accept her offer, but it seemed the most practical solution as far as caring for Olivia was concerned, and in Riley's mind the child should be the prime consideration.

He'd been OK until she'd reached out to take off his cap, Mitch decided as he walked towards his room to obey Olivia's instructions. Sure, her vibrant hair had been featuring in his dreams, and his body had been doing a bit of unfamiliar stirring whenever Riley Dennison was around.

But he could put that down to the 'when did he last have sex' thing—thanks, Clare, for the reminder!

However, when Riley had swayed closer, and her fingers had moved towards him, he'd seen the action in slow motion, and had felt the shape and softness of her as clearly as if he'd been holding her in his arms.

'Weird stuff!' he muttered to himself. 'Maybe it was to do with the haircut, although Samson lost his strength, not his mind!'

Though it *had* been a woman's fault, he remembered darkly.

He pulled a suit and a couple of clean shirts out of the cupboard. Remembered Riley's remark about not doing laundry and added two more shirts.

Underwear, socks, shoes for work and casual, a pair of casual trousers, casual shirts, sweater. What else would he need?

'Don't forget your toothbrush.'

He swung towards the door but she'd already disappeared, no doubt to haunt someone else for a few minutes.

His mood didn't improve as he followed the truck Riley drove towards her father's house, although when he saw the position, in daylight, high on a hill looking out over the ocean, he found himself relaxing slightly.

Olivia, who'd opted to drive with her new-found friend, raced straight inside as soon as the truck stopped, but Riley waited for him, leaning back against the cab and looking out over the water.

'I never tire of it,' she said, waving her hand towards the view. 'So utterly beautiful.'

Mitch found himself agreeing, although he was looking at the woman, not the vista spread before them. The marvel of what she beheld had softened her face and darkened her eyes so, with the waving mass of hair, she looked like someone out of a Renaissance painting.

'Well, come on in,' she said, breaking the spell. 'I'll show you your rooms. It's a huge house so you can be as private as you like.'

She led the way up shallow steps and into an entrance with corridors leading off to the right and left.

'It was built so every room gets a view,' his guide explained. 'To the left are the living and dining areas, and the kitchen, where we spend most of our time. Up this way, there's Dad's rooms first—he's got an office in there and his own bathroom, then my bedroom and bathroom, then two more bedrooms separated by a third bathroom which you and Olivia can use.'

'Three bathrooms? That was rare in an older house.'

He saw the pride in Riley's face as she took the words as praise.

'Dad built the house when he and my mother were first married. They planned to have a lot of children and my mother insisted on the bathrooms. She'd grown up with six brothers and sisters and always had to share.'

She opened a door as she spoke and waved him into a spacious room, tastefully decorated in shades of blue. It had a vast double bed, and also a comfortable-looking armchair and a small television set.

All the comforts of home.

Mitch dropped his bag and turned towards his benefactor.

'I'm very grateful to you and your father for putting us up. It will definitely be better for Olivia than being in a hotel.'

He paused, wanting also to apologise for his grouchiness, to explain it was the accumulation of misfortune that had upset him, but the words wouldn't come. And an inner uncertainty, unlike anything he'd ever felt before, made him feel grouchier than ever.

'Perhaps I could take you and your parents out to dinner,' he suggested. 'Save your mother cooking.'

The lovely eyes, today reflecting the green of the T-shirt she wore beneath the overalls, gave him a considering look.

'My mother died in childbirth,' she said quietly. 'My father brought me up, which is why he's well qualified to look after Olivia.'

She turned and walked away, leaving Mitch staring after her.

He wanted to ask why, and how. To protest that such things didn't happen these days, although he knew, from time to time, they did.

And he wanted to comfort her. To hold her in his arms—

Delete that thought, Hammond! Hang up your clothes, then go and see the real Riley to thank him for his hospitality. Repeat your offer of dinner.

Do anything but think licentious thoughts about the red-head while you're a guest in her father's house!

He shut the door, hung up his clothes and put socks and

underwear into a drawer. Turned on the television and discovered it was set to the channel playing the football game he kept missing. Perhaps he could watch a little of it.

He slipped off his shoes, pulled back the bedcover and, spurning the chair, lay down on the bed to enjoy what remained of the game.

The sensation of being watched, of not being alone, brought alertness, and one glance around the dark room told Mitch he'd slept. He turned his head and, in the light from the corridor, saw the watcher. Pyjama-clad, and clutching against her chest the dog-eared book she favoured these days as a bedtime story.

'Riley said you must be very tired to sleep so long, but I knew you wouldn't want to miss my story.'

He held out his arms and Olivia raced into them, snuggling up against him, clinging with little limpet arms.

'Of course I wouldn't want to miss your bedtime story,' he said, whispering the words against her newly brushed and baby-scented hair. 'That's the one thing I most truly hate when I'm called out to work.'

And as he said the words he reacknowledged in his heart just how precious his daughter was to him.

'Do you want to show me your bedroom?'

She took his hand, huffing and puffing as she pretended to pull him up off the bed, then led him past the bathroom to another large bedroom.

'Riley lent me some of her old toys,' Olivia announced.

'Only some?' Mitch said faintly as he surveyed the menagerie spread across the double bed. It was as far removed from the fairies and dolls of her bedroom at home as he could imagine. 'Is there any room in there for a little girl?'

Olivia chuckled, then dashed towards the bed to show him exactly where she fitted.

Mitch was still dubious.

'Are you sure they won't frighten you if you wake up in the night?' he asked, moving a giraffe so he could sit down to read the story.

Blonde curls waved vigorously around her head as she denied this.

'They're my friends. They'll protect me.'

She slung her arm around the neck of a virulent green crocodile and nodded for her father to start the story.

Riley Dennison, the female one, was waiting in the hall when he finally emerged after moving enough animals to tuck his sleeping daughter under the blankets.

'I found this night-light. She might like it beside her bed. And if we leave the hall light on she'll be able to find you without too much trouble if she does wake in the night.'

The words were calmly spoken and eminently sensible, but they captured less of Mitch's attention than the woman who spoke them. For the first time since they'd met she wasn't wearing overalls, though jeans and a casual shirt weren't so different. Except that the jeans clung to legs as long as for ever, and the shirt, in some kind of knit material, emphasised pert but softly rounded breasts.

And she smelt of apples and cinnamon instead of wood shavings...

'I've kept your dinner hot. It's in the oven. Go that way and you'll find the kitchen. I'll fix the light.'

Thus dismissed, he walked away, telling himself it was all Clare's fault—not to mention the accident which might be in part to blame, and possibly a mid-life crisis brought on by the problems at his house.

Was thirty-four too young for mid-life crises?

But throughout these cogitations the image of the reed-slim woman with the abundant glory of hair remained riveted in his mind.

And his body remained on full alert for her return.

'You'll find an oven cloth hanging on a hook above the bench,' the real Riley Dennison informed him.

The man was standing in the kitchen, pouring freshly made coffee from a pot.

'I've a pile of work to catch up with in my office, so if you'll excuse me…'

Mitch nodded at the already retreating figure. The thank-you speech he'd mentally prepared would have to wait. But at the door Riley senior hesitated.

'Don't worry about your house,' he said. 'If I'm not back on my feet when Riley starts her other job, Jack's said he'll take over. He's a fine young builder. Should be. I taught him myself.'

And on that cryptic note, which undoubtedly was meant to make Mitch feel better, he departed.

Mitch found the oven cloth, opened the oven and all but drooled when the delicious aroma wafted out.

'It's a vegetable pie,' the female Riley's voice said from behind him. 'There's a salad to go with it in the refrigerator, and knives and forks in the top drawer.'

She was standing on the far side of a big kitchen table, waving her hands to indicate what was kept where.

And telling him, at the same time, she had no intention of waiting on him.

Which suited him, he assured himself.

He set the plate on the table, found the salad and the cutlery he'd need, then hesitated. Sitting down to eat alone at the big table made him feel uncomfortable. Especially with the woman standing opposite him.

'I assume you've eaten,' he said, 'but would you like to sit a while? Perhaps have a cup of tea or coffee?'

She grinned at him.

'It's horrid, being in someone else's house, isn't it?' she said, surprising him with her percipience. 'You always feel

uncomfortable, no matter how hard you try to fit in and be
unobtrusive.'

He felt her gaze skim over his body.

'Not that unobtrusive is quite the word to describe you,'
she added obscurely, but he was pleased when she poured
a cup of coffee, added milk, then carried it to the table and
sat down opposite him.

'What happened to your mother? Do you know? Did you
ever want to find out?'

He wasn't sure why he'd asked the question, but learning
things about Riley Dennison suddenly seemed important
and, for him, it was a natural place to start. He cut into his
pie and began to eat, giving her time to decide if she wanted
to talk about it.

She didn't reply at once, sipping at her coffee, studying
him over the rim of the cup as if to fathom why he'd
brought it up. Then she shrugged.

'Of course I wanted to find out. Apart from anything
else, I'm a woman, and with the genetic inheritance it could
have been something I had to take into consideration myself.'

'And was it?'

She shook her head and her cloud of red-brown hair
moved, shimmering in the light, tempting him to forget
about medical subjects and pursue more personal ones.

'As far as I can gather, she had a long labour. Probably
longer than a doctor would allow these days. In the end I
was delivered by Caesarean, and within a day my mother
had developed a high temperature and obvious signs of
infection.'

'Metritis?' Mitch suggested. 'Have you heard that
word?'

She smiled at him.

'Heard it and looked it up. Are you sure you want to
talk about this over dinner?'

She nodded towards the meal he was demolishing with relish.

'Sure!' he said. 'Doctors who find it difficult to discuss all but the most extreme of revolting subjects over the dinner table would probably starve to death.'

She nodded to show she'd accepted his assurance, took another sip of coffee and continued.

'Once I decided I wanted to know, I went into it quite extensively.' She set down the coffee cup and glanced his way. 'It's funny the things you remember. I guess I was only twelve or thirteen, yet I can recall reading that, like most pelvic infections, two types of organisms are present. Polymicrobial, the book called it, then the article went on to explain it meant both aerobic and anaerobic microbes were conspiring in the infection.'

'What did you look it up in?' Mitch asked. 'That's fairly detailed info.'

Again he saw the ready smile which lit Riley's face with a teasing delight.

'One of my uncles worked at the hospital. He was like my father, who always believed you learned more by working things out for yourself than by having someone tell you. He sneaked me into the hospital library and I went from book to book. I kept having to go back to the dictionary to find out what different words meant, but the aerobic and anaerobic stuck because I knew them from basketball.'

Mitch looked blankly at her. Polymicrobial and basketball?

'From exercise,' she explained. 'Aerobic and anaerobic exercise. The words were familiar because in training we did aerobic and anaerobic exercise. Of course, there was much, much more I read that I've forgotten.'

'But your mother died as a result of the infection?' Mitch shook his head. 'It seems impossible even—how old are you?'

'Twenty-eight,' she said promptly, apparently unaffected by a question many women would have refused to answer.

'Well, twenty-eight years ago, I would have thought broad-based antibiotics were sufficiently powerful to have fixed metritis.'

He considered what he would have done in such a case—initial treatment with intravenous administration of a combination of clindamycin and gentamycin, then, if symptoms persisted after forty-eight hours, a different combination of antibiotics to cover the pathogens not susceptible to the original drugs...

'I'm sorry,' Mitch said into the silence that had lengthened as he'd thought it through.

'Don't be,' she said, the smile again teasing at the corners of her mouth. 'I could practically see you writing the prescriptions. What did happen was that an abscess developed, and although these days either ultrasound or imaging technology would probably pick it up, back then no one did and she died of the infection.'

Mitch felt the weight of sympathy fill his chest, but couldn't express it.

'Tough on you,' he murmured, feeling he had to try.

'Far tougher on my dad, who'd not only lost the woman he adored and was left as sole support for a squealing, squalling scrap of humanity who must, at times, have seemed to him to be the cause of all his problems.'

'And she still is,' a gruff voice remarked, and Mitch glanced up to see Riley senior come into the room. 'I'm heading for bed. You'll walk the dogs?'

This last question was obviously directed at his daughter, and the kiss the man dropped on the top of the russet curls told Mitch she wasn't enough of a problem for him to have stopped loving her dearly.

'I'll walk the dogs,' the woman promised. 'Goodnight, dad.'

Mitch saw the silent interaction between the pair, the visible love and genuine affection in which they held each other, and he wondered if it would be the same between himself and Olivia.

One day!

He finished his meal and stood up, taking the plate to the sink and, with some difficulty given the restrictions of the sling and hard collar, washing it under hot running water. As he looked around for a teatowel, one hit his shoulder, thrown by the woman who was watching his clumsy efforts with a teasing smile lighting her eyes.

'Given your injuries, I'd do it for you, but it's my belief you're already far too spoiled. And I know the sling is only to remind you not to use the shoulder too much, not because you're in dire pain.'

'As if you'd care,' Mitch grumbled, but the homely routine of drying his plate was strangely comforting. Reminded him of his childhood, when the obvious shortcomings in his mother's vague attempts at maintaining hygiene had meant he'd done the dishes throughout his formative years.

And quite enjoyed the thinking time it gave him.

'Have you finished with the cup?' he asked, when Riley stood up and stretched her sinuous body so unselfconsciously he wondered if she was aware of how attractive she was.

She passed it to him, then asked, 'Have you everything you need? There are clean towels in the bathroom, books in the living room. Can you think of anything else?'

He sensed she was only waiting for a reply before disappearing out of his life. For today at least.

And much as he'd wished her to the moon on various occasions, now, tonight, he didn't want that happening.

'Then if there's nothing else,' she said, obviously giving up on him answering, 'I'll be off. I want to give the dogs a decent walk before I go to bed. Poor Henry's trying hard to be a good father, but he does get bored with hanging around the house all day. Usually he's on the truck with Dad, and he misses the outings.'

You're explaining too much, Riley told herself, but although she, too, was longing to get out into the crisp night air, she was reluctant to leave Mitch alone in the kitchen.

Not that she didn't trust him. It was more that she sensed a loneliness in the man. As if the problems of the last few days had finally slammed him up against realities he'd been loath to face.

She studied his face and saw, as well as strain, the laugh lines at the corners of his eyes, and the easy tilt to his lips as he gave her a half-teasing smile and said, 'May house-guests join the dogs for a walk?'

'I guess so,' she replied, her heart leaping with delight while her inner guardian tried to squelch such excessive reaction with reminders that it was only a walk. 'But it will be cold. You'll need a coat.'

He strode away as if the prospect of walking two energetic Labradors was a high treat, and Riley moved more slowly, snagging her own jacket from the hook behind the kitchen door and shrugging into it. As she walked outside, Henry, knowing what was in store, bounded up, and Betty, not willing to be left behind, eased herself away from her sleeping puppies and leapt nimbly out of the enclosure that kept the pups from straying.

Mitch appeared, the dark suede jacket he'd slung across his shoulders making him look bulkier, its collar hiding, or almost hiding, the stiff collar.

He fell in beside her as she walked around the house.

'Henry and Betty?' he exclaimed when she introduced the dogs. 'How on earth did you come up with those names?'

Riley chuckled.

'Before this pair, we had Wendy and Brad. Only-child

syndrome, wouldn't you say? If I couldn't have siblings, I'd have dogs that sounded like people.'

She heard his answering laugh and felt a warmth that defied the brisk wind blowing in from the ocean. Felt other things as well, as if tiny fibres were connecting their bodies so that as they walked in the beauty of that star-filled night, along the headland above the glimmering, glistening sea, she was wrapped in a special kind of wonder.

The dogs bounded along in front of them, dashing off into deep shadows then reappearing, returning now and then to gambol around their human companions, then racing off again to investigate new scents and sounds.

'I've been wasting this place,' Mitch said, speaking quietly so the words seemed in harmony with the soft shushing of the waves on the beach below them. 'Here but not here. Uncaring of the beauty, forgetful of the simple pleasures of a walk along a headland.'

He stopped and turned to face her, taking her arm to hold her still.

'Thank you,' he said, and the depth of his voice, an echo in its tone, made her pulse still, then race, then hiccup into panic as the links she felt between them imbued the moment with an anticipation so extreme she could feel her body trembling for what was to come.

He leaned closer, and in the moonlight she could see his eyes, intent on hers, his lips moving as if preparing for a kiss. Skin taut with need, she waited, her nerves alert to every nuance of movement in his body, then he stepped away, striding on towards the cliff-top, calling to the dogs who, with a total lack of discrimination—or feeling for their mistress—gambolled after him.

Damn, but that was close, Mitch thought as he stared down towards the waves, surging and gurgling around the base of the cliff. He could all but taste those tempting lips, experience their freshness, feel their silky texture on his skin.

He'd been mesmerised by the sheen of moonlight on her cheeks, the wild profusion of vivid, vibrant hair. Had felt his body drawn towards hers as if by some invisible force between them, until one second more of moonlit madness and he'd have been kissing her.

Kissing Riley Dennison?

The aggravating woman who, whichever way he looked at it, had caused him more problems than a dozen wives and wreaked more havoc in his house than an earthquake?

The no-sex thing must have him tied in knots. Or something she'd put in his dinner had affected him.

A single bark from one of the dogs—he needed to be closer to distinguish which was which—made him turn, in time to see Ms Dennison bounding down the grassy slope towards the beach, her hair streaming out behind her as she leapt the small bushes in her path.

And something in the freedom of her movements, the sheer joy with which she ran, made him want to follow. To shout, 'I'm coming.' And go hurtling down behind her, catching up and grabbing her in his arms, swinging her aloft in exultation.

'Stop right now!' he told himself, speaking aloud in case some part of him might misunderstand the warning. 'For a start, you don't know this hill as well as she obviously does, so you're likely to fall over and make a total ass of yourself. *And* rick your neck again, not to mention your shoulder, and probably end up in hospital. And if you're unlucky enough that neither of those fates befall you, then you might take into consideration that while moonlight and Riley were a powerful combination to resist, moonlight and water and Riley might prove your undoing.'

He listened very carefully to these sage warnings, nodded to himself to show he'd heard them, then, with only slightly less abandon than the woman had exhibited, he headed down the slope.

CHAPTER SEVEN

LOOKING back on it later, Riley wondered how a simple walk along a beach could have left her so tightly wound that her nerves were still snapping several hours later. She tossed and turned in bed, desperately seeking the oblivion of sleep, hoping it might unravel the coils within her.

When she'd fled the tension of the strange interlude on the headland, the last thing she'd expected had been for Mitch Hammond to follow her. But, no, he'd had to come flying down the hill only minutes after her, oblivious to his injuries, or the risks of doing further damage to his person.

And though she'd scolded him for his foolhardiness, all he'd done had been to laugh, then settle on a rock to remove his shoes and socks and roll his trousers up to his knees.

'Come on,' he'd said to her. 'Now we're on the beach we might at least paddle.'

Which was when she'd thrown caution to the winds. She'd paddled with him, the dogs chasing the curling frothy edges of the waves, bounding around the pair as they'd splashed along the wet sand and through the shallow water.

'It's like time apart,' Mitch had said, reaching out to take her hand and hold it in a warm, firm clasp. 'A slice of unreality—a dream.'

Content to go along with such a fantasy, she walked with him, and when, in the shadow of the rocks, the entwining strands of emotion she'd felt earlier once again caused that strange tension in the air, she wondered if he'd kiss her.

Almost hoped he would.

But Betty began to fret about her offspring, and whined

and danced around them. The real time and the real world intervened, dampening down the fires and fancies as effectively as the water the two dogs sprayed from their coats dampened her clothing.

'Get down!' she told the dogs, when Henry joined the game. 'Come on. I'll take you home.'

Mitch didn't argue, merely saying, 'I might walk some more.' Then he strolled off along the sand as if that 'slice of unreality' he'd conjured up had never been.

'Well, if he can pretend it never happened, so can I,' Riley told herself, and she snuggled deeper into the bed. 'Normal! That's what tomorrow will bring.'

But though she spoke valiantly, she knew it was a lie. Something within her was changed for ever by that strange moment when they hadn't kissed, yet she could imagine it so clearly—the taste of his lips, the feel of his body against hers, the sight of his eyes, intent in the moonlight.

You must have been out of your mind to have even considered kissing her! Mitch told himself, waking in the strange bed and remembering the even stranger interlude they'd shared the previous evening on the beach.

Yet the temptation of her lips had haunted his dreams, and the way he knew her body would feel in his arms had him stirring even now.

Fortunately, Olivia, catapulting into the room, brought some sanity back to his life, and as he gravely responded to her introductions to the assortment of animals she'd brought with her, he worked on getting his life back into perspective.

'Hello, Harold,' he said politely to a particularly ugly hedgehog, while inwardly acknowledging that, OK, he *was* attracted to the female Riley.

'Natural enough as she's an attractive woman,' he told

Harold while Olivia went to collect more 'friends' for him to meet.

'But to get involved on a permanent basis?' he said to Blanche the bear—or was Blanche the rabbit and Roland the bear? He shook his head.

'No way,' he told them both, picking up the ones that fell as he moved off the bed. 'No way! She's a disaster area. The kind of person trouble follows down the street. Been there and done that with my whacky family, whom…' he lifted Roland—or maybe it was Blanche—and looked at him—or her—in the eye '…I love very dearly, it's just that I can't live with them.'

Olivia returned with the crocodile and giraffe.

'I need order in my life,' he explained to his daughter. 'I like things calm and under control.'

'What's "under control" mean?' Olivia asked, setting the giraffe and the crocodile on the edge of the bed.

He knelt and gathered her in his arms and held her close.

'Everything that my life isn't right now, sweetheart,' he whispered, then he tickled her and they wrestled until she tired of the game and departed, announcing in a parody of adult habit that she had to visit her puppy now but she'd play with him again later.

Mitch showered and dressed, in casual clothes. He wouldn't go in to work straight away. Right now, it seemed more important to check what was happening at his house.

A taunting voice suggested it had more to do with who was likely to be at the house than what was happening there, but he ignored it. After all, there was no guarantee Riley would be working with the pest exterminator. In fact, it was unlikely she would be.

And even if she was, now he'd thought about it rationally—without moonlight and water—and fully understood she wasn't the woman for him, the attraction would surely die away.

Thus fortified, he made his way towards the kitchen, but before he reached the door he realised if he went further he'd be interrupting an argument. And the fury with which Ms Dennison was arguing served to prove he'd been right about her attracting trouble.

'Of course you have to tell him!' Riley senior was saying, and through the small opening Mitch could see a flushed-faced demon in faded blue overalls glaring furiously at her father.

'I do not have to do anything of the kind!' she stormed. 'He'll find out soon enough and I deserve the chance to argue my case directly, and not with preconceived barriers already raised against me.'

Was she worried someone would turn her down for a job on the grounds of her gender?

It had probably happened to her more than once.

Mitch walked away then started back again, treading more heavily so they'd hear him before he reached the door.

Not that it mattered, as she'd gone by the time he reached the kitchen, and only a slight frown on Riley senior's face betrayed evidence that a storm had passed that way.

He carried it off well, offering Mitch a choice of cereals, telling him Olivia was outside with the dogs and that Riley had gone down to his house to let the exterminators in.

'I'll go down later myself,' Mitch said. 'They may need stuff shifted. If I'm off work I might as well be doing that.'

The older man nodded and passed him milk and sugar, offered coffee from a pot that smelt freshly made. Yet he was hesitant, as if he wanted to say something but didn't know what words to use.

Mitch chatted easily about nothing in particular, as he did with patients when he first met them, giving them time to size him up and feel comfortable in his presence. But it didn't work with Mr Dennison, who in the end left the house to join Olivia and the puppies.

Mitch cleared away the breakfast things, then sought his daughter.

'Come on. Time for a wash then off to pre-school for you.'

The pout appeared, but the miracle that was this new Olivia remained, for all she said was, 'Do I *have* to, Daddy?' Once there would have been a tantrum.

'Of course you do,' he told her. 'Won't all your friends be waiting to hear about the puppy?'

The pout changed to excitement and he congratulated himself on handling it so well, then realised where he'd picked up this new approach to his daughter's behaviour and silently admitted something good had come out of Riley Dennison's eruption into his life.

He dropped Olivia at the centre and went on to the house. Thanking Riley for this revelation might be a good way to get over any awkwardness from the previous evening.

Though there wouldn't be any awkwardness if she hadn't felt the same tension he'd experienced.

Whatever she may or may not have felt was a moot point, as she wasn't there to be thanked.

'She let me in, cleared some food out of the kitchen and took off again,' Michael told him. 'She might be up at the timber yard, ordering what she'll need to replace the timber in the walls, or down at the hardware, getting sheeting.'

Mitch sensed Michael had several more suggestions about where Riley might be, so he cut the man off with a polite thank you and departed.

'Supervising the job and she's not even there!' he muttered to himself as he drove away, although he knew he should be pleased, not angry.

With nothing else to do he went to work, where Clare expressed surprise but then admiration of his new look.

'Really suits you, the cropped look. Very handsome!' she assured him, then spread the word that he'd finally had a haircut around the offices so colleagues kept dropping in to see for themselves.

He escaped to the lunch room, but those who hadn't already seen it soon followed.

'Hmm!' Harry murmured, walking all around him to view the new Mitch from all angles. 'Usually when a man improves his image to this extent—and it does suit you, mate—there's a woman somewhere in the picture!'

'Haven't you lot got anything better to do?' Mitch demanded, annoyed by his own discomfort at Harry's remark. It had been the barber's mistake, and nothing to do with the woman!

He herded Clare, who'd now joined the fun, back towards their suite of offices.

'Have you any appointments lined up for a temporary housekeeper?' he asked, when she'd passed him the morning mail.

She shook her head.

'One agency had a woman who'd come in afternoons to mind Olivia and cook your dinner, but that doesn't solve your on-call problem and you can't expect Harry to continue doing night calls.'

'No, you can't,' Harry told him, walking in at that precise moment and perching on Clare's desk. 'In fact, I've been meaning to remind you about Friday week. It's Jenny's show opening and you're definitely on duty that night, my friend.'

Mitch assured his partner he'd hold the fort, although how, he hadn't quite figured out. By Friday week, with any luck, he'd be back in his own home, but that was going to make child-care arrangements worse, not better.

Harry, apparently appeased, departed, while Mitch, leaf-

ing through the mail, found a demand for participation in
a pre-school bring-and-buy stall.

'I definitely need a wife,' he muttered to himself, as once
again the difficulties of single fatherhood threatened to
overwhelm him.

'Don't we all?' Clare said, and the echo of the sentiment,
if not the words Riley had used, startled him. He leafed
through more mail, wondering, for possibly the first time,
how women managed to juggle jobs and families and the
million and one things 'being a wife' entailed.

'But at least you can do something about it,' Clare said.
'Find yourself one.'

The idea was so startling he had to stand still while he
examined it.

It was the obvious solution, but his heart quailed at the
effort it would involve. He had no idea where, in a town
he didn't know well, one should begin the search.

And when his mind strayed to memories of a moonlit
beach, he reined it firmly back into line, walked through to
his office and kept it from straying again with some serious
paperwork. Nothing like wading through governmental red
tape to ruin thoughts of romance.

Although, thinking of the beach, Riley Dennison *was* a
local. She might be able to point him in the right direction—tell him where to go to meet some single women.

She'd be more likely to tell him where to go, full stop,
if he dared to enlist her help!

He'd reached this point in his thoughts when his phone
buzzed.

'Blythe Reid is here,' Clare told him. 'I know you're not
seeing patients but she's upset and doesn't want to talk to
Harry.'

'Send her in,' Mitch answered without hesitation. Blythe
had been referred by a community social worker, and
though he took many patients, free of charge, from the

community aid group each year, this young girl-woman was somehow special.

And very woebegone, he realised as she came through the door, collapsed into a chair and released the sobs she'd been holding back.

Clare, who'd followed her in, looked anxiously at Mitch, but he waved her away, then called after her, 'Perhaps a warm, milky drink of some kind, Clare. Have we got some drinking chocolate?'

He came around and perched on his desk, waiting for the worst of the tear-storm to subside.

'Want to tell me about it?' he asked gently, when Blythe finally raised tear-drenched eyes towards him.

She didn't answer. Shook her head, and blonde curls, not unlike Olivia's, swung around her shoulders.

Mitch continued to wait, wishing for more skill in counselling—or perhaps a magic wand he could wave to make the world come right for vulnerable youngsters like Blythe.

'I told my mum and dad.'

The whispered words were so brittle that Mitch felt his heart crack. He stepped forward and squatted down by the chair, taking Blythe's hand in his.

'I knew they wouldn't want to know,' she continued, her fingers grasping his as if he were a lifeline back to sanity. 'But you'd said I should tell them. That maybe they'd help.'

The bleakness in her voice told him how wrong he'd been.

'So, what do I do now?' she whispered, and once again raised her head, her piteous eyes meeting his.

'You'll be OK,' Mitch assured her, straightening up and giving her a pat on the shoulder. 'It really doesn't change things all that much, now, does it? They might have been a help if you chose to keep the baby, but now they've opted out we have to think of other help you can get. Other support for you. It's not all bad, Blythe. In fact, sometimes knowing where you stand makes things easier.'

He could see she didn't believe him, and his arms ached to take her in his arms and comfort her, as he would have done with Olivia if she was hurting.

But professional ethics meant he had to stand apart. He could supply practical help but not the good hug she desperately needed.

Clare returned and put down a tray with a steaming mug of chocolate and a plate of biscuits.

'Here, love. Have something to eat and drink. You'll feel much better with something in your stomach.'

Then Clare did what he couldn't. She put her arms around the young woman and hugged her, patting her shoulder, smoothing her hair and murmuring loving nothings until Blythe straightened in her chair and once again looked like the pretty, healthy teenager she was.

She sipped her chocolate, ate a biscuit, thanked Clare, who departed, then looked at Mitch.

'I'm not upset about my parents. I kind of knew they'd say exactly what they did say.'

The candid blue eyes that were looking directly into his suddenly filled with tears again.

'I'm upset because I know the sensible thing would be for me to have an abortion and yet I can't bring myself to do it.'

Mitch swallowed the lump that formed in his throat, coughed to make sure it had gone, then cleared his throat again for luck.

'You've a few more weeks before you have to decide,' he said gruffly, then, like a beam of light from above, an errant scrap of information slotted into place in his head. The woman taking Peter's place had experience in teenage pregnancy counselling. 'And before that, there's someone who might help you think through the decision.'

Blythe began to protest, but he held up his hand.

'I know you've seen the counsellors at the community centre, but they're so overworked they don't have a lot of time to give to every individual, no matter how hard they try. This person will be working here from next week.' That pre-empted a decision! 'If I make an appointment for you, will you see her? Talk to her before you decide?'

The young woman nodded, then, looking far more cheerful—perhaps because decision making had been adjourned for a while—she finished her chocolate and ate another biscuit, smiled radiantly at Mitch and departed.

Clare came back in to take the cup and plate.

'Miracle-worker strikes again?' she teased. 'I didn't think she'd ever smile again, yet she was positively glowing as she left.'

Mitch shrugged.

'I suggested she talk to this Susan who's taking over from Peter. Didn't you or he or someone say she'd be working with him next week?'

The startled look he got from Clare puzzled him momentarily, but he was so pleased to think he might have found someone to help Blythe make her decision, he didn't dwell on it.

He phoned Peter's secretary instead, wanting to deal directly with her so he could impress on her the need for an urgent appointment and offer to pay for the consultation if the new person didn't want to take on *pro bono* work.

Feeling pleased with himself, he tackled more forms and files, finally declaring himself up to date at lunchtime. He'd go home and check on the destruction there. See for himself exactly how many holes had been drilled in his floor.

Remembering what Michael had said about Riley clearing food out of the kitchen, he bought a sandwich and a cool drink on the way. If he had a wife, would she make him lunch? It wasn't something Celeste had ever done but, then, she hadn't even been out of bed when he'd gone to work. And Mrs Rush was always busy getting Olivia up and organised…

With his mind mulling over the possible advantages of marriage, he turned into his drive and parked behind the now-familiar truck his 'builder' was using at the moment.

'Don't go inside,' a voice called, and he looked skyward to see the overall-clad figure sitting on the high ridge of his roof.

Without considering any other option, he clambered up the scaffolding, with some difficulty, and joined her, taking a minute to assimilate the beauty of the view, then un-wrapping his sandwich and twisting the top off his drink.

The empty lunch wrappers told him she'd also chosen this vantage spot to eat, but it wasn't food he wanted to discuss with Riley Dennison.

'You're a local. Where would I go to meet single women?'

Riley was glad she was sitting down—she'd have fallen off the roof for sure if she hadn't been.

'Desperate, Dr Hammond?' she asked, hoping her teasing tone hid the inexplicable ache beneath her breastbone.

'No, I'm not desperate,' he snapped. 'But surely there's nothing unreasonable in a single man deciding he'd like to meet some single women.'

Riley shrugged.

'I guess not,' she admitted.

'Well?' he persisted, and she had to think back to the original question.

'I haven't lived here for seven years and when I do come home I come to see my dad, visit friends, catch up with people I know. I don't do the singles scene, so I can't help.'

'But you must have heard of places people go,' he said, and she turned to look at him.

Caught him watching her, his brown eyes intent.

'You might not be desperate, but you seem very keen all of a sudden,' she said. 'Did demolishing the shrine break the last tie to the—your wife?'

He glared at her.

'That room was not a shrine!' The words held enough venom to poison a snake. 'Setting it up like that was Mrs Rush's work. For some reason she must have decided the fancy dresses were too delicate to be hung in cupboards. Or perhaps she did like to see them strung around the place. I had no idea they were there.'

Riley held up a hand to ward off his wrath.

'OK, OK,' she said. 'Let's not get into roof rage! Anything could happen!'

He laughed at that, and seeing him, be-collared but laughing, did more than start an ache beneath her breastbone. It started palpitations in the region of her heart. Surely she was too old to be falling in love.

And she was definitely too set in her ways to even consider a relationship.

'Well, if you can't point me in the right direction for meeting women, who can?'

The question reinforced her determination to not get involved with this man. For a start, he obviously didn't see her as a 'woman'—certainly not as a desirable one—or he wouldn't be asking about where to meet more of her gender.

'Haven't you friends or co-workers who'd introduce you to women? Wouldn't that be more dignified than hanging around the singles scene—advertising that you're desperate and dateless?'

'I may be dateless,' Mitch growled, 'but I am *not* desperate!'

There was a pause and she guessed he was, with difficulty, getting his temper back under control.

'This is purely a business decision. I've known for a long

time women prefer married obstetricians. I've had a period of grace since Celeste left, but now seems an opportune time to consider remarrying.'

'And if you're really quick—do a whirlwind courtship thing—you might also solve your problem of a temporary housekeeper!'

The glare he'd delivered earlier was nothing on the thunderous scowl he turned on her now.

'You can make light of it,' he stormed, 'but one look at the statistics on marriage breakdown these days should be enough to convince any sane person that marriage needs more than all the dewy-eyed romance stuff so widely touted as "true love". Marriage as a sound business arrangement makes a lot of sense.'

'Perhaps you could advertise for someone,' Riley suggested. She'd realised that joking about this was by far the easiest way to handle the inner unease it was causing her. 'Woman wanted to enter into marriage partnership—no romance required. You'd probably get a flood of applications from women who'd already gone down the "true love" road and found it ended in a bramble patch.'

He peered suspiciously at her.

'You're laughing at me!'

She grinned at his injured tone.

'Not entirely,' she told him. 'I'm sure there are plenty of women who'd be happy to enter that kind of arrangement. You're not bad-looking—well, once you get rid of the collar—and you've got a house, a good income, stability. What more could any woman want?'

Love? her heart whispered, but she knew Mitch couldn' see into her heart, so she was safe.

'So how do I go about finding one?' he asked, and though she contemplated pushing him off the roof, in the end she went for practical.

'If you don't like the idea of advertising, then network. Use your friends—'

'I can't ask my friends to find a woman for me!' He sounded so horrified Riley set aside a momentary peevishness that he'd ask her, and hastened to reassure him.

'You don't have to ask!' she said. 'I'm quite sure, back when people realised your wife wasn't coming back, they were always inviting you over and foisting single women on you.'

The look in his eyes told her she was spot on. Not that she'd needed confirmation—well-meaning friends had been 'finding men' for her for years.

'Then you probably dropped out. Stopped going to their parties, and the invitations eventually dried up.'

He nodded. 'But that doesn't help now,' he told her.

'It does if you get yourself back into the system.' She thought for a moment, then said, 'You could start by giving a party.'

She'd barely said the words and he was glaring at her again.

'You're suggesting *I* give a party? Have you forgotten a little matter of a termite-ridden house, no housekeeper, a roof about to come off, tiles missing off the walls? The place is in chaos and I'm supposed to give a party?'

'There you are—being negative again.' Riley gave him a glare of her own. 'By Friday you'll be back in your house with no sign that the termites have ever been there. With this delay, the roof definitely won't come off until the following week. You can use the little setback you've had as an excuse. Throw a "farewell-to-the-termites" party. Make a joke of it, for heaven's sake!'

'And how is my throwing a party going to introduce me to single women?' He was dangerously calm now. 'Should I advertise in the local paper? Single women welcome to attend?'

Riley heaved a huge sigh and shook her head.

'Don't you know anything about social interaction? Even the basic rules?'

He didn't reply so she told him.

'Rule one is you always have to return invitations! Once people have been to your place, they'll all start asking you back. And apart from maybe a once-a-year big bash, most couples these days entertain by having dinner parties and they never invite odd numbers to dinner parties so they'll—'

'Invite a single woman to make up the numbers?'

He sounded slightly calmer now, and even nodded as if he was following her reasoning.

'But that could take ages!' he objected, and she realised she'd been congratulating herself too soon. 'I'm hardly likely to be asked to a dinner party every week. Once a month if I'm lucky. Then a month or so to get to know each candidate—it could be a year or more.'

'There's no need to sound so horrified,' Riley snapped. 'If you'd started a year ago you mightn't be so desperate now.'

Which brought them back to square one.

'I am *not* desperate!' he repeated gruffly, and shuffled down towards the scaffolding.

'Then please yourself how you go about it!' she yelled after him. 'All I was trying to do was help!'

She watched him disappear from view. Of all the peculiar conversations she'd had with Mitch Hammond, this one took the cake! But helping him find a wife wasn't such a bad idea. It was blatantly obvious he had no interest in her and, given the strange twinges she was feeling in his presence *and* the fact they'd soon be colleagues, the sooner he was married and therefore off limits to her or any other woman, the better.

In the meantime, she had a house to set in order.

The sooner he was back home, the better, too. Inviting him to stay had been a very bad idea.

CHAPTER EIGHT

MITCH might have scoffed at Riley's suggestion, but as he climbed back down the scaffolding he began to wonder if she wasn't onto something.

He had a good backyard, a wide deck and a big barbecue. An informal farewell-to-termites party might be the very thing. And barbecues had been his favourite way of entertaining—back when life had seemed so much simpler.

Though he wouldn't for a minute consider such a devious and extremely long-term ploy as a means of getting himself a wife, a party might be fun!

By the time he reached the ground, the idea had taken hold.

Forbidden to enter his own home and unwilling to make a nuisance of himself by returning to the Dennisons', he drove back to work. He could think about it there. He also had to check with Clare about the housekeeper situation. Surely the agencies had some interviews lined up for him by now.

'The afternoon and early evening woman is the best anyone can do,' his secretary told him. 'But she has a family of her own and won't sleep over.'

He bit back an oath of frustration—after all, it wasn't Clare's fault.

'I might be able to get a high-school student to sleep over,' Clare added. 'It's only for a few months, until Mrs Rush comes back.'

'Great idea,' Mitch told her. 'See when the afternoon woman can come in to meet me and we'll take it from there.'

He went on into his office and pulled out a notepad. He'd make a list of people to invite to the barbecue—another list of food he'd need. Celeste had always bought salads already made up—Clare would know where to get them.

Everyone from work—well, Peter wouldn't be able to come. He was going north to see his parents which was why his farewell party had been last weekend.

Riley Dennison?

Well, it had been her idea, and she was one of those organising type of females who'd probably be useful to have around. And he did owe her and her father a favour for having him and Olivia to stay. He'd ask them both.

He added Riley and Riley Senior to his list and smiled to himself. That way, she'd have someone to accompany her and he wouldn't have to ask if she wanted to bring a partner.

By the time he left the office he had a list of twenty-four, mostly colleagues. Those he saw he invited on the spot, then grew increasingly aggravated at their responses.

'A party? You?' Tracey said.

'What's the occasion? A symbolic rebirth? Return to life?' Harry teased.

Jill offered to do whatever she could to help, and Clare gave him a most unsecretary-like hug and said, 'Welcome back, boss!' Then kissed him on the cheek.

The positive responses heartened him and he returned to the Dennisons' bursting with enthusiasm, intending to thank Riley for her suggestion and perhaps talk over his embryonic arrangements with her.

'She's not here, lad,' the older Riley said.

'She's fixing up our house and wearing a mask so she doesn't get sick.' Olivia expanded on the information. She hugged and kissed her father then led him outside to inspect the birds. 'I don't want her to fix it too quickly,' she confided. 'It's nice here with Mr Riley and all the animals.'

Mitch felt a stab from something he assumed must be his conscience. Had life been so dull for his daughter that she was relishing the company of a middle-aged man and his birds and dogs?

'You'll have your own dog before long,' he reminded her. 'And maybe we can get some birds if Mr Riley will teach you how to look after them.'

'I already know,' Olivia told him. 'They must have fresh water and food every day and you have to keep their cages clean and give them nice fresh seeds and grass and things to chew on.'

Mitch listened to her explanations and walked along the aviaries where the birds flew happily among small shrubs and specially planted grasses, but he was conscious of a nagging wish to be inside the house—or wherever the other Riley might be.

So he could produce his list and say, See, I'm not incapable of running my own life?

Or for some other reason?

But when they did finally go back inside, it was time for Olivia's bath, and when that was done her dinner was ready—the plate waiting in the microwave, a note indicating what to do to heat it slightly.

Voices from Mr Dennison's office suggested the younger Riley had returned, but no doubt she had business to conduct with her father.

Mitch told himself it was stupid to feel disappointed. All he'd wanted to do was show her his list! He read Olivia her bedtime story and tucked her into bed, then walked back out towards the living area of the house, feeling ill at ease again—intrusive.

'Dinner's ready. I'll eat with you. Dad's gone down to the club.'

Riley's brisk decisiveness helped, but it also set her apart, as if some barrier had been erected between them.

They ate, conversing politely, and when he mentioned that he'd adopted her idea of a party she nodded, but he sensed his affairs were the last thing on her mind.

'I'm not doing it as a way to eventually meet some single women,' he told her, thinking maybe she'd only been joking when she'd suggested it and now was offended by his deviousness.

'No, but if you want to meet some, it might work. And if you want to speed up the process, make it an open house. Tell people to feel free to bring a friend or two.'

'Would you?' he asked, and Riley, deciding she'd better get with this conversation, frowned.

'Would I what?'

'Bring a friend or two? Perhaps a special friend?'

'Are you saying you're asking *me* to this party?' she said, not sure seeing him in a social environment was a good idea.

'Why not? It was your idea.'

She stared at him, then remembered just how the party idea had come up.

'You're back to that, aren't you? Only now you're expecting me to line up some single women for you?'

And for all she knew it made sense to get him married off, the thought still hurt.

'It's not as bad as you make it sound,' he protested. 'Just that most of the people there will be work colleagues and you might not know many people. I thought you'd be more comfortable if you brought a friend. And, of course, I'll ask your father.'

'And ask him to bring a friend?' Riley demanded.

She finished her dinner and stood up to take the plate across to the sink.

'Anyway, he'll be in hospital,' she muttered, then to her utter amazement, and mortal embarrassment, she burst into tears.

Desperate to escape before Mitch caught sight of this pathetic behaviour, she abandoned the plate and hurried through the back door. And once enveloped in darkness, she was able to wipe her eyes on the sleeve of her shirt and blow her nose instead of sniffing.

'What's wrong?'

She'd been so busy mopping up the tears she hadn't heard him come out, and now the gentle caring in his voice and the steadying support of his hands on her shoulders started them flowing again.

'I'm being stupid,' she said, the words muffled by her handkerchief. 'I know perfectly well he'll be all right, and that he needs positive people around him at the moment, and I'll be positive when I'm with him, it's just—'

The hands on her shoulders forced her to turn, then, when she was facing him, shifted in such a way that she was drawn close against Mitch's broad chest, and his arms closed comfortingly around her back, his hands patting her in a reassuring manner.

'Bad news about your dad?'

She nodded against the conveniently placed shoulder.

'About his back?'

She nodded again, then shook her head.

Realised the shoulder was too convenient for her peace of mind, and stepped out of his embrace.

'Apparently it's not his back. He's had back trouble for so long he assumed it was and decided a week's rest would fix it, but the pain was different and he had other symptoms he has no intention of discussing with his daughter so in the end he went to see his doctor. He has a tumour on his right kidney and the urologist thinks it will have to be re-moved—the kidney, not just the tumour.'

'People survive with just one kidney,' Mitch said, his voice as reassuring as his hands had been earlier.

'I know that much,' Riley told him. 'It's the long-term prognosis that bothers me.'

The medical phrase prompted Mitch to review what he knew or could remember of kidney tumours. Not much that was good, but Riley didn't need to know that right now.

When he'd had to deliver bad news, his policy had always been to stick to practical matters as much as possible. He tried it now.

'So when's he going into hospital?'

'They're admitting him tomorrow. He has to have scans and tests but apparently it's easier for the specialists to do them with him as an inpatient than to have him running back and forth.'

'And they can start feeding fluid into him as well,' Mitch told her. 'That's essential before any kidney operation. It flushes out any poisons in the system before invasive surgery begins.'

'It's serious, isn't it?' Riley said, and the pain in her voice caused an ache in Mitch's heart.

'Not necessarily so,' he said, hoping he didn't sound falsely hearty. 'Have they done a biopsy, do you know? Perhaps that's what they'll do when he goes in. Take a little bit of it and test it.'

'Without operating?'

Mitch tried to think. So much of his work was done through what was commonly called keyhole surgery, he imagined kidneys could be approached the same way.

'Without major surgery,' he said. 'They'll use a long needle, like a probe, to draw up a few cells—they don' need much. Then run cytology tests—check the cells fo any differentiation that will show malignancy.'

His right hand was still resting on her shoulder so he fel the shudder rip through her body.

'It could be benign,' he added. 'Particularly if only one

kidney is affected. I think kidney cysts are usually unilateral.'

'And if it's not benign?'

She was looking directly at him, and though the light was dim he knew she would detect any evasion.

'If it's a malignant tumour then, yes, if it's not caught early, it could have spread throughout the abdominal cavity and that's bad news. But as I said, the kidneys are also prone to cysts—benign tumours that may have some malignant cells in their walls but once removed cause no further problems.'

Riley nodded, then, with his eyes now adjusted to the moonlight, he saw her smile.

'Thank you,' she said with grave dignity. 'I'm glad you were here. Talking about it makes it all slightly more believable. Definitely less frightening.'

She whistled, and Henry appeared from the darkness.

'Come on, boy. Let's walk.'

Mitch wanted to go with her, but sensed she needed to be alone so he crossed to the pen where Betty was patiently waiting for her pups to finish their evening feed, and he leant down and stroked the golden head.

Back inside, he washed the dishes and tidied the kitchen, pleased with this new domesticity he was showing. Although his party plans had lost their appeal now Riley wasn't around to discuss them with him.

He watched a little television but in the end went to bed, though he didn't sleep until he'd twice heard the back door—the favoured means of entering or leaving the house for both Rileys—open and shut.

'Olivia and I will shift into a hotel. There must be a vacancy somewhere,' he told his host the following morning when he wandered into the kitchen to find Olivia eating breakfast with the older man. 'You certainly don't want the bother of extra people in the house with the worry of hospitalisation and possible surgery.'

'Don't even think about it,' Riley replied. 'By Friday your house will be back to rights and that's when you move, not before. You're starting back at work today but Riley will be here to mind Olivia when she finishes at preschool this afternoon. When you're on night duty you can have your phone calls diverted, and if you're called out at night you'll not be worrying.'

Mitch didn't want to argue with him, particularly not in front of Olivia, but if he'd felt bad about being under an obligation to these people earlier, he felt worse now.

'And don't be thinking you're a nuisance,' Riley continued. 'I'm grateful it all happened this way. Having the two of you in the house will take my lass's mind off her worries over me.' He hesitated then said, 'We've been closer than most fathers and daughters. I guess you'll find that, too, with this wee mite.'

The wee mite chose that moment to fall off her stool and the ensuing fuss meant Mitch couldn't refute the man's excuse—or explain why he felt they should move on. Instead, he comforted his daughter, searched for blood, applied a plaster strip anyway, dried her eyes and finally oversaw the pre-departure routine and took her off to preschool.

And although it wasn't far out of his way to drive by his house and check on what was happening there, he didn't, proceeding directly to the hospital for a round of his and Harry's patients.

'She probably wouldn't have been there anyway!' he muttered to himself.

'OK, who's first in line?' Mitch asked Clare, when he arrived at the rooms an hour later.

'Mrs Martin. She's a new patient, referred by Dr Warren.'

Clare handed him the file. David Warren was a GP in one of the hinterland towns west of Port Anderson and regularly passed on clients to the practice.

Mitch made a note to invite him and his wife to the party. They had two little girls about Olivia's age who'd be company for her.

Perhaps he'd need a high school girl to keep an eye on the kids. He made another note to ask Clare's advice on this.

Then decided to get down to work and opened Mrs Martin's file.

Apart from the standard files the practice used, on which Clare had entered the basic details of name, date of birth, address and private health cover, it consisted of a single letter from the referring doctor. It was short, sweet and to the point.

'Small-town stuff happening here, Mitch,' David had written. 'Mr Martin has been dead for five years and Mrs Martin tells me she can't be pregnant but I suspect she is. She came to see me because she'd decided she was menopausal and wanted to discuss hormone replacement therapy. Palpation of her abdomen revealed a soft, swollen uterus suggestive of about eight weeks gestation which would fit with the two missed periods. However, the "can't possibly be pregnant" statement meant she was unwilling to undergo any further tests. Leapt at the idea of a referral.'

David had signed the letter then added as a postscript, 'Virgin births not being common out this way, it'll cause a stir.'

Mitch considered the implications for a moment, his eyes idly scanning the information Clare had entered on the new file.

According to the date of birth Mrs Martin was forty-five.

And had never had children.

That in itself was enough to cause him some concern.

He buzzed and Jane, their young nurse, brought Mrs Martin in, then tactfully withdrew.

'I'm Mitch Hammond,' Mitch said, holding out his hand to the neat, small, beautifully groomed woman who'd entered.

'Nancy Martin,' she said, and the smile that wobbled on her lips reminded Mitch of Blythe Reid. Age didn't take away all uncertainty!

'So, how can I help you?' Mitch said.

She studied him for a moment, her dark eyes searching his face.

'I guess I need to know first,' she said, 'and then we'll go from there.'

'Know if you're pregnant?' Mitch said gently.

She nodded, shrugged, then shook her head.

'It's so impossible I can't get my head around it. When David suggested it I was outraged. I mean, it seems so vulgar, someone my age having a baby.'

'It happens more and more these days,' Mitch told her, but Nancy Martin wasn't easily diverted.

'Not unless people are really trying, and more often than not using fertility pills or some physical intervention.'

Mitch smiled at her.

'Not so in your case?'

She rolled her eyes.

'Far from it. It was the last thing on my mind. I mean, I was married for twenty years and didn't conceive—why on earth would it happen now?'

'From the way you're talking I assume it's not totally beyond the realms of possibility.' He hesitated, then walked across the delicate ground. 'You are in a physical relationship?'

Mrs Martin blushed and looked out the window, then she turned back to Mitch.

'I can't talk about that,' she said firmly.

'Because being pregnant will cause complications?' Mitch guessed.

'I might not be pregnant,' she countered, though he couldn't tell from her voice if not being pregnant would be good or bad.

Maybe she didn't know herself.

'But you want confirmation?' Mitch asked her. 'Want to know one way or the other?'

She sat for a moment, then nodded. 'I could have done it myself, I guess, with a pregnancy kit, but first of all it didn't occur to me, and then when David said—' She broke off, then smiled as she continued.

'I reacted badly to poor David's suggestion it might be possible. I behaved like an outraged virgin! It was shock more than anything, but heaven knows what he thought.'

Mitch returned her smile.

'I can imagine the shock,' he said, and waited. This was a woman grappling with more than just the idea she might be pregnant, and he didn't want to rush her.

'What do you have to do—to confirm it?'

'Various things,' he told her. 'A urine test—that's easy as far as confirming pregnancy is concerned. But some of the sample will be used for other pathology—things like the presence of sugar, renal function and evidence of urinary-tract infection. My nurse will take blood for a full blood count, blood grouping, tests for any antibodies you might be carrying.'

Mrs Martin nodded as if she was accepting all of this so Mitch continued.

'I'd like to do a pelvic examination, which will give me some idea of gestational age, and also bring to light any possible problems you might encounter later. I'll do a pap smear at the same time. Then an ultrasound which even at this stage will detect evidence of the baby's heartbeat.'

'What about other tests? To see if it's all right?'

'Amniocentesis? We do that later.'

'I might not want the test,' she said, surprising Mitch as much as anything had since he'd read her age.

'It's up to you,' he said, 'but it's not something we need worry about now.'

'OK, let's find out for sure,' she said, and Mitch buzzed for Jane to come back in.

'Jane will take you through to an examination room and take the samples we need. She'll also take your blood pressure and pulse so we know where we are, then introduce you to the instruments of torture we keep around our examination tables. They look far worse than they are so try to relax. I'll be along when you're settled.'

He would normally use this time to jot down some notes on the patient's file, but he had no idea what to make of Mrs Martin. No idea if she was going to be happy to have this pregnancy confirmed. Or if she intended going through with it. Though she'd brought up further tests and said 'might not want' amnio, not 'might not need'.

Thinking about it didn't produce any sudden illumination so he walked through to the examination room where his patient was now gowned and covered by a light blanket as she rested, most uneasily, he was sure, on the high table.

'Do I have to put my feet in those things?' she demanded.

'It makes it easier for me, and, I'm assured, more comfortable for you.'

She grumbled but let Jane lift her feet into the stirrups.

'Definitely pregnant, Mrs Martin.' Mitch watched her face as he spoke but she closed her eyes and he couldn't tell if the news was good or bad. 'Nine weeks, I'd say, but we'll work out dates later.'

He talked to her about her general health, which apparently was, and always had been, good, then he left Jane to help her dress and went back to his office where he buzzed Clare.

'How long before my next patient?' he asked.

'Ten minutes, but it's Mrs Embry for a postnatal check and if Jane does all her preliminary stuff first, you could have twenty.'

'Organise it for me, could you? This may take a while.'

When Mrs Martin was shown back in, he waved her to a chair then held up his hand to stop Jane leaving.

'Would you like a cup of tea or coffee?' he asked his patient, and was pleased when she summoned up a smile.

'Don't you offer anything stronger?' she said, and he chuckled.

'Not to pregnant women,' he told her firmly. 'Tea? Coffee?'

She shook her head and he nodded to Jane who went quietly out the door.

'At this stage I usually counsel my new patients about their health and diet, cautioning them against smoking, drinking alcohol and the dangers of any other substance abuse. We discuss family medical history and routine prenatal care, what symptoms to expect, what symptoms should cause alarm. The signs of possible complications, that kind of thing.'

'Usually?' Mrs Martin seized on the word.

'Not all my patients are happy to find they're pregnant,' he said, deciding this was a woman who'd appreciate plain talk. 'For them, my prattling on about not smoking, as if being pregnant was the most wonderful thing in the world, could cause them more distress.'

He waited for a moment, then said, 'I'm here to help those people as well as the others, you know. Here to listen, to answer questions, to advise if it's within my field of expertise.'

'And does deciding what to do next—whether to keep a baby or have it aborted—fall within that field of expertise, Dr Hammond? Do you have a formula for telling a married man you're pregnant with his child? Or, for that matter, do you provide words for a middle-aged woman who's never had a child to use when she tells her friends she's pregnant?'

The woman's voice was robust, lacking the whine of self-pity, and Mitch smiled at her.

'I think you'll find all the words you need,' he said. 'When and if you need them. Right now, the main concern is you. You have to decide what *you* want to do. A pregnancy at your age could be difficult, although your general health is good so you could sail through it. But there could be complications, so if you remain under my care I'd want to see you more often than I might see a twenty-five-year-old expecting her first child.'

'Doctor's visits I can manage,' Mrs Martin said, then she smiled at him. 'But I think my health was the least of the things you feel I should consider. I don't seem to be thinking too well, so what are the others?'

'Your health is the prime consideration as far as I'm concerned,' Mitch contradicted. 'But for you, the question is whether or not you want this child. Kids aren't like pets that we see in a shop and choose because they're cute and cuddly and will fill a void in our lives. They're yours for life and often they're not cute and definitely not always cuddly. You have to consider the financial aspect of having a child, of feeding and educating him or her. Can you afford a child without becoming resentful of the cost of it?'

Mrs Martin nodded as if to show she was considering all he said.

'I can afford a child,' she said quietly.

'That's good,' Mitch told her. 'Then there's something else that's more important still. You have to consider the emotional nurturing the child will require—the freely given and unconditional love it will need to grow up whole. Have you got that love to give? Would you want to give it to a child? To this child in particular?'

'Who better?' Mrs Martin said, and when she looked at Mitch he saw the soft glow of happiness which had replaced the bewilderment in her eyes.

'You don't have to decide today,' he told her. 'Take a few days, a week, think it through. Phone me if you have any questions.'

'Would you do a termination?' she asked and as ever the question, valid though it was, was like a punch to his stomach.

'Under some exceptional circumstances I have performed terminations,' he said carefully. 'However, from a purely personal point of view—not medical or religious, just personal—I'd prefer not to. But if you decide that's what you want, I can refer you to an excellent woman doctor who does do it.'

His patient studied him for a moment, then said, 'That's fair enough. I'll go away and think about all of this.'

Her voice was bleak now, and Mitch realised the happiness had gone from her eyes. He didn't want her walking out like that and asked gently, 'The man with whom you're having the relationship—can you talk to him? Discuss this with him? Would that help you decide?'

'The man with whom I'm having a relationship, as you so carefully phrase it,' she said, 'is the most wonderful man in the world and, yes, I could talk to him about it and discuss it with him and no doubt he'd help me decide, but what I don't know is whether it's fair to add to the burdens he's already carrying. To cause him more pain than he's already suffering.'

She looked directly at Mitch and said, 'Sometimes truth causes more trouble and heartache than a lie or an evasion, doesn't it?'

And Mitch, because he'd been thinking of Celeste and the baby he hadn't known she'd aborted until after the fact, nodded his agreement.

He stood up and held out his hand to help Mrs Martin to her feet.

'If there's anything I can do to help,' he said, 'let me know. Clare will give you an appointment card. It has my home phone number on it as well, so phone me any time you want to talk.'

'You surely can't make that offer to all your patients,' she said, and Mitch smiled at her.

'Only to very special ones,' he said, and thought he saw a hint of that glow of happiness return to her eyes.

But as he examined the latest little Embry his mind kept returning to the woman who had so much to decide.

Peter's successor had experience in counselling pregnant teenagers. Although far removed in age, Mrs Martin's dilemma was much the same.

'He's a grand little boy, Mrs E.,' he said, but he was thinking Friday couldn't come soon enough. He wanted to meet this woman and, if she was any good at all, get her installed in the building. Pregnancy counselling was valid whatever age a woman was.

Blythe Reid and Nancy Martin—two women as far apart in years, nature and circumstances as the north and south poles, yet caught in similar circumstances at this point in time.

Would a support group of some kind be a help...?

CHAPTER NINE

THE rest of the day passed without incident, women in various stages of their pregnancies, filing through the door, some filled with joy at the approaching event, others suffering the discomforts of swollen feet and indigestion, wanting only for the forty weeks to be up.

Hoping Mitch might tell them they'd deliver early!

All commenting on his collar, and teasing him gently about his trendy new haircut.

At five, Mrs Marshall appeared, sent by the agency.

She was large and jolly and very enthusiastic, and Mitch, when he'd talked to her for half an hour and had found nothing he could object to in her manner or the answers to his questions, agreed to start her on a trial basis on Monday.

'Perhaps you could come over on Sunday so Olivia has a chance to get to know you,' he suggested.

'Of course I will,' Mrs Marshall said. 'Nine o'clock?'

Mitch nodded and it was only after she'd departed he remembered about the party and wondered if perhaps nine was a little early.

Though Olivia would certainly be up and about by nine so he guessed he would be as well.

Now all he had to do was get someone to sleep over each night and he'd be right.

He sighed as he considered this next task. A wife was becoming a better and better idea.

Solve the sex thing as well. For some reason, that part of his body, which had been reasonably quiescent since Celeste's departure, was returning to life—reacting most inappropriately at times.

He'd have to remember to include regular sex in the marriage agreement. No doubt a wife would expect it anyway but it was best to have things spelled out.

The juxtaposition of thoughts of sex and a wife proved distracting, and it was only with difficulty he dragged his mind back to work-related matters.

He had no one due to deliver for a couple of weeks, but arranged for his calls to be switched to his mobile anyway and, after writing a short note to David Warren, confirming Mrs Martin's pregnancy but saying nothing else, he left his office and drove out towards his house.

It was forty-eight hours since the place had been treated. Surely he could go in now.

He unlocked the door and walked cautiously inside. The chemical smell hung heavily in the air, and he was tempted to forget any further exploration.

Hell! He'd invited dozens of people to a barbecue on Saturday afternoon—the place had to be presentable by then. Holding his handkerchief over his nose and mouth, he ventured forth. Kitchen first.

Big mistake! If anything, it looked worse than it had on Monday morning when he'd last seen the place. Sawdust had been added to the general mess and now lay like thick yellow dust over every surface.

'I'll kill that woman,' he muttered to himself, then remembered that right now she was doing him a huge favour by minding his daughter. He amended the threat. 'Next week, when I have a housekeeper.'

But the thought led to other thoughts, to Riley's tears and how strong yet pliant she'd felt when he'd held her in his arms. He got back into his car and drove on to the hospital. He'd visit Riley senior, find out who was treating him, perhaps glean some information that wouldn't be passed on to the family.

It was the least he could do by way of repayment.

*   *   *

'We've got to go,' Riley said to Olivia. 'Your father will come home and wonder where we are.'

'No he won't,' Olivia declared, batting the balloon, which she'd insisted Mr Riley would love, back up to the ceiling. ''Cos he's here. He's in the hall, talking to the nurses. I saw him when I got some water.'

Riley closed her eyes and told her stomach to settle and her heart to behave. Last night he'd held her to comfort her, nothing else, but could she convince her stupid body that was the case?

'We'd best be off, Dad,' she said, bending to kiss her father on the cheek. 'If Dr Hammond's here it probably means he's forgotten where we hide the key and can't get into the house.'

Her father smiled, seeming more relieved than dispirited by the idea of their imminent departure.

'I'll call you as soon as I hear anything, but the specialist was almost sure the tests would show a cyst. Apparently they put dye into me next and the final scan tomorrow should clear up any doubts. He even apologised for throwing a scare into me.'

Riley grinned at her father.

'He'll have to do more than apologise for the scare he threw into me,' she said. 'Maybe some grovelling would do for a start.'

'Grovelling?'

Trust Mitch Hammond to come in right on cue! Fortunately, Olivia's enthusiastic reaction to her father's presence saved Riley from explaining.

'Are you going straight back to our place from here?' she asked him, when order had been restored.

'If that's all right with you,' he said, sounding more uncertain than she'd ever heard him.

'Of course,' she assured him. 'I was only asking because

Olivia might like to stay with you. I'll go on ahead and start dinner.'

'Can't I take you out?' he protested. 'It's bad enough dumping ourselves on you the way we have, but you certainly don't have to feed us.'

'We could go to McDonald's,' Olivia suggested, jumping up and down with delight at the idea.

'I'd much rather cook,' Riley assured them both, then she said goodbye to her father once again and left the room.

On Friday Mitch would go back to his house, so all she had to get through was this evening and the next. Two short segments of time—not impossible, surely.

And what about the 'meet the other tenants' thing Clare had told her about? And then working in close proximity to the man?

She told herself it would be OK, especially once he remarried, but her heart grew heavy at the thought and she wondered if working anywhere within a hundred miles of him would be too close.

One worry at a time, she decided. Tonight first.

All she had to do was cook a meal and eat with him. That shouldn't tax her acting abilities too much.

Olivia helped. Excited about the party her father was planning, she chattered non-stop, pausing only to seek confirmation or approval from one or other of the adults. And after dinner Mitch took his daughter off to bed, while Riley restored the kitchen to its usual neat order. Light rain made walking the dogs impractical, and she was standing in the kitchen, wondering if there was anything worth watching on television, when Mitch reappeared.

'Your father's prognosis seems much better than you'd thought,' he said, and she nodded, pleased because he sounded genuinely interested in her father's health. 'I spoke to his urologist and he feels if it proves to be a cyst he can remove it without taking out the kidney.'

'Thanks for doing that,' Riley replied, realising their guest had made a special effort to see the specialist.

'Hey, I'm the one who should be saying thanks,' Mitch said lightly. 'Though I'd be saying it far more enthusiastically if my house looked even vaguely livable.'

He came right into the kitchen, and seemed to draw all the air from the room so she was left breathless and shaky.

'You can move back in on Friday,' Riley promised him, steeling herself against the increasing weakness in her body. She filled the kettle, more as something to do with her hands than for any other reason. 'Would you like a cup of tea? Coffee?'

'Coffee,' he replied, taking the kettle from her hands and switching it on. 'You sit down. I'll do it.'

But Riley couldn't move, her body too heavy to lift, her knees too weak to carry the weight. So he worked around her, getting cups and milk, finding the instant coffee and a teaspoon, totally unaffected by the whatever affliction she was suffering in his proximity.

It can't be love, an inner voice wailed, but she suspected it could be. Unless it was some dire disease with extremely bizarre symptoms that had crept up unannounced and struck her down.

Then sanity returned. Whatever it was, she had to get over it. The man was in the market for a wife, but it was abundantly clear he didn't consider her as a possibility.

And she certainly wasn't aiming for wife status—not with a man to whom love was a not particularly attractive four-letter word.

She forced her feet into motion and made it to the far side of the breakfast bar, where she slumped gratefully down on a stool.

'So, how's the wife-hunt going?' she asked, just to prove to herself she understood the situation.

'It's hardly a wife-hunt!' Mitch objected, setting down a

cup of coffee in front of her then pushing sugar and milk in her direction. 'Simply a move in the direction of a common-sense arrangement.'

There was a small silence, then he added gloomily, 'And it isn't going. I doubt this party thing will work and, really, the more I think about it, do I really need a wife?'

'List the advantages,' Riley suggested. Chatting about hypothetical wives was infinitely preferable to sitting brooding over the man.

'Someone at home at night when I'm called out,' he said, and she had to laugh.

'That's it? That's the prime consideration?'

He turned an affronted look on her.

'No! It would be good for Olivia and I'd have someone to keep the little things organised, like finding a replacement for Mrs Rush.' Then he brightened. 'Actually, I've done that. Or Clare and the agency and I, between us, have done it.'

He told her about the woman he'd interviewed, mentioning she wouldn't sleep over.

'Then you've still got a problem,' Riley pointed out.

'I think Clare's looking after it,' he said. 'A high-school girl.'

Mitch saw the frown and wondered what on earth he'd said wrong this time. Talking to Riley was like wading through a creek you didn't know—you never knew when you were going to end up beyond your depth.

'Something wrong with a high-school girl?'

She grinned at him.

'Not on principle,' she said. 'Or perhaps it is in principle that there's a flaw. Mothers of teenage schoolgirls tend to be protective of their chicks.'

A series of thoughts clicked into place.

'Bloody hell! Are you implying a girl could be in moral danger, sleeping over at my house?'

'No,' Riley said quickly, while an earnestness in her lovely eyes repeated the denial. 'She'd be more likely to be harmed by gossip—as would you. I might be wrong, but unless this town has changed since I last lived here, I don't think it's such a wise idea.'

'But Clare suggested it,' Mitch protested.

'She was probably desperate to get you off her back,' Riley told him, then she chuckled. 'Or weren't you nagging at her to find you someone?'

He scowled at her so she didn't think she'd read the situation correctly, and then he groaned.

'What the hell am I supposed to do?'

'Hurry the wife-hunt?' Riley suggested glibly, and he gestured threateningly towards her.

Then, although strangling her was what he'd mimed, he remembered the feel of her shoulders, the fine bones beneath her flesh, and his fingers tingled with a need to touch gently, to feel her shape and form and pliancy once again.

'Definitely hurry the wife-hunt!' he muttered, and made for the back door. He knew Riley senior kept a raincoat on a hook in the shed. He'd put it on and walk the dogs—cool off!

Lusting after a woman while a guest in her father's house was inappropriate, to say the least. And she'd not shown the slightest interest in him. In fact, she had a distressing tendency to prod and poke at him, to argue and irritate and incite him to anger. Hardly indications of romantic interest!

He found the raincoat and pulled it on, then whistled to the dogs, but although Henry came to investigate the sound, he gave Mitch a look that suggested only idiots walked in the rain and retreated to his warm, dry kennel.

Faced with the option of walking alone in the rain or returning to the kitchen where, he now remembered, he'd left his coffee untasted, Mitch dithered. The shrill summons of the mobile in his pocket meant he could delay the decision.

He answered and Mrs Martin introduced herself.

'How long do I actually have to think things through?' she asked, then gave a little laugh and said, 'Talk about dispensing with the formalities. How are you, Dr Hammond?'

Mitch also laughed.

'Forget the formalities,' he told her. 'Beginning with the doctor-thing. Call me Mitch, and to answer your question, a termination in the first trimester, that's the first twelve weeks, is the easiest and safest. You've three weeks to think about it if you want to go that way. But it's also possible to perform one further into the pregnancy with little risk to you. Terminations for medical reasons—'

'You mean because there's something wrong with the foetus?' Mrs Martin put in.

'Yes, or for the health of the mother. These are often done later—right through the second trimester, up to twenty-four weeks.'

'I couldn't wait that long,' Mrs Martin whispered. 'Couldn't stand the uncertainty. I have to decide now, before it tears me apart.'

'Can you give me until Friday?' he said gently. 'There's a new psychologist in town who has experience in pregnancy counselling. She's dealt mainly with teenagers but your situation isn't all that different.'

Mrs Martin laughed softly.

'Not all that different at all!' she confirmed. 'Yes, I can wait until Friday. And I'd be very grateful if the woman would agree to talk to me. I can't seem to think straight by myself.'

Mitch found his heart grow heavy with pain for the woman. From the way she spoke, she loved the man who'd fathered her child. He hoped she'd find some way through the maze.

Hoped the psychologist would live up to her CV and glowing references.

And be willing to see Mrs Martin as soon as possible.

Though he couldn't recommend her until he'd met her. Friday!

He strode off down towards the beach, pleased to have found something to distract his mind from Riley Dennison—the female one. Though when he reached the headland, he remembered the tension he'd felt between them on that other walk and he wondered if she'd felt it.

'Probably totally oblivious to it!' he muttered to himself. 'And she'd laugh at you if she knew what you were thinking.'

But a sense of her presence remained with him, so he walked with her ghost by his side, and he said things to it he wouldn't have said to the person.

By the time he returned she'd gone, though a light in the study suggested she might be working late. Mitch watched television for a short time then went to bed himself, tapping on the study door to say goodnight as he walked past.

Sleep was a long time coming, and when it did come, a long, lean lissom female kept parading through his dreams and causing so much turmoil he woke unrefreshed—edgy and out of sorts.

'Riley's gone to work,' Olivia told him, when he came grumpily into the kitchen. 'She's going to finish fixing the bits the termites ate at our house today, and do some painting tomorrow and then we can go home.'

Bright blue eyes gazed up at him.

'Do you want to go home, Daddy?'

'Most definitely,' he said, perhaps too forcefully if the sudden dimming of the brightness was any guide. 'We like our house, and all your toys are there,' he said, but the bottom lip was now starting to tremble and he had to give her a hug and hold her for a while to assure her—and inwardly himself—that they'd be OK.

'There's the party to think about,' he reminded her as he restored her to her stool.

'But I'll miss the two Rileys,' Olivia told him. 'And the animals and birds.'

'You can come and visit often,' Mitch promised, then hoped Mrs Marshall would be happy to oblige as far as visiting the Dennisons was concerned. His internal warning system was suggesting, forcibly, that the less he saw of Riley, the more settled his life would be.

'Riley said that, too,' Olivia told him, then she added sadly, 'But it won't be the same.'

He knew it was a child's form of emotional blackmail, but felt the guilt nonetheless. Since the advent of Riley into both their lives, he'd been made aware of the lack of— well, fun in Olivia's life. She'd been well cared-for, and dearly loved, but beyond that? How often had he played with her? Taken her to the park? Invited her friends over to play?

'You'll have the puppy soon,' he reminded her, but he vowed he'd do better. And finding a wife was becoming even more urgent. He'd need one who liked children and got on well with them. Someone who would bring some fun into his daughter's life.

They did the morning thing and he dropped her off at pre-school, checking out the staff there—all female but far too young.

Where else did females congregate?

The hospital? Full of nurses, still predominantly female.

He did his ward round with a new attitude, taking a new interest in the women with whom he came in contact nearly every day.

Nurses, he decided, came in all shapes and sizes, and

had varying degrees of beauty and attraction, but none he'd noticed actually attracted *him*. It was becoming obvious that once you dropped out of the dating game, getting back into the groove might prove very difficult.

'I've found a high-school student willing to sleep over on your nights on duty.'

Clare greeted him with this news, and Mitch remembered Riley's reservations.

'Riley says…' he said, and then he smiled, thinking how he'd resented his daughter's repetition of that phrase.

'I know what Riley says,' Clare told him. 'I've known Riley Dennison since we went to school together. She's not one to keep her opinions to herself.'

Clare chuckled, as if remembering some particular incident, then added, 'And she was right, although I hadn't thought of it. There could have been all kinds of complications. Imagine if the poor lass had fallen in love with you!'

'You don't have to make that sound like some dreadful fate,' he grumbled, then recalled what they should be discussing. 'So how did you and Riley solve it?'

'I found a lad. Gary Wheeler. He's the oldest of six so is good with younger kids, very sensible. His mother teaches at the primary school and his father's a farmer. Their property is about twenty kilometres out of town. Good family. He'll be perfect. He's actually delighted as he's in his final year and sleeping over a few nights in town means he can spend some time in the library after school and do some extra study.'

Mitch felt relief wash through him. Another problem solved.

Then he remembered something else Riley had said.

'When can I meet him?'

Clare grinned at him.

'I've asked him to pop in after school. Mrs Wheeler will

come, too. I guess she wants to check you out as much as you want to check him out. Could we get the bus to drop Olivia here? After all—'

'I know!' Mitch said. 'She has to be happy with him as well. Could you phone the pre-school and arrange it? And let Riley know she's coming here.'

He mentally reviewed these most satisfactory arrangements, then added, 'And tell her I'll take Olivia out for tea, so not to bother cooking for us. I'd take her out as well, but she keeps refusing and I think her father's due out of hospital today so it will give them a bit of time on their own.'

Clare nodded, and began to look as if he was keeping her from her work.

Mitch took the hint and headed contentedly for his office. Maybe life wasn't so bad after all.

Definitely not so bad, he decided much later when Gary Wheeler had been met and approved by all parties concerned, and Mrs Wheeler had pronounced Mitch responsible enough to employ her son.

Gary had agreed to come over on Saturday afternoon to help Mitch set up for his party, then keep an eye on the children while the parents relaxed. He'd even volunteered to organise some games, and had totally won Olivia's heart by offering to include Pass the Parcel.

Now Olivia was tucked up in bed, Riley senior had protested tiredness and had also retired, leaving him and the other Riley to walk the dogs.

The rain had cleared, leaving the stars freshly washed, spangling in an immense wine-dark sky. The moon was a huge yellow orb lifting itself slowly from the sea, and the soft wind blowing through Riley's abundant russet hair was carrying the scent of it to Mitch's nostrils.

It was a night custom-built for romance, he decided, and

wondered how the woman with him might feel about the subject when she broke the silence.

'So, what will you do once you meet a candidate for wifedom?' she asked.

Well, at least that answered his question of how she might feel about romance!

'What do you mean, what will I do?' Disappointment sharpened the words, but sharp words held little threat to Riley Dennison.

'Just that! What will you do? How will you court her? You must be a bit out of practice at the dating game. Where will you start?'

She was striding along, the dogs loping in front then falling behind. And firing questions at him as if this was just a casual conversation.

Disappointment swung towards aggression—how could he possibly have been thinking of romance with someone so aggravating?

Although the question did bear some consideration. He hadn't, until now, thought past the actual finding of some available woman.

'I'll take her out to dinner.'

Riley hooted with mirth.

'How predictable!' she chortled. 'Oh, what fun she'll have!'

'It will give us an opportunity to get to know each other.'

'Very important,' she mocked, and he swung towards her, grabbed her shoulders and glared down into her face.

'What would you suggest I do? Walk her on a headland? Wait for the moon to rise? Then take her in my arms and kiss her? Like this, Riley?'

He claimed her lips, and although the kiss started out as hard and angry, it became something else he couldn't quite describe, so he broke it, stopped and lifted his head. Then he looked down into her silvery eyes and said, more softly, 'Or this?'

She'd provoked him into that first kiss, Riley realised, with what little brain-power she'd retained after the force and urgency of it. But not this second one.

This second one was more an exploration, and when a heat, like a lit fuse, began deep in her belly, she explored in turn and felt the fire streak through her body until she wondered what kind of conflagration might follow if she and Mitch ever seriously kissed.

Meaning it.

For this wasn't serious, the remaining bit of brain still functioning told her body. This was anger and frustration and a lot of other things all boiling out of Mitch.

She just happened to be there.

But as she was…

She stopped thinking, giving in to the magic of the night, to the warmth of his embrace, the temptation of those lips that had gentled in their force yet still demanded, and persuaded—and tempted her to join the fun.

For what seemed like for ever they stood, locked together in a fierce embrace. His hands had left her shoulders and were moving across her body, firm and strong, pressing fingers into her flesh as if he needed to know her the feel of her bones. And her own hands crept around his neck and her fingers felt the prickle of newly cut hair, the feel of the hard, well-shaped skull beneath the skin, sensations at once so different yet enticing she could feel her nerves tingle in response.

Her body fitted neatly, felt his warmth and fed her own to him in return. Punishment, if that's what it had been, had turned to promise—but what he could promise wasn't what she wanted, she remembered, and reluctantly let go and drew away.

She felt her knees wobble with an enervating weakness, and only utter strength of will kept her upright.

He'd been teaching her a lesson—taunting her for being cheeky. No way could she let him guess her reaction to what was, after all, just a kiss.

Just a kiss? her mind shrieked, but she ignored it and conjured up more strength.

'Well, that might work,' she said, hoping the words sounded flippant enough to fool him. 'An unusual approach perhaps, but there's a certain charm in novelty!'

He didn't answer, contenting himself with a glare strong enough to be obvious in the moonlight, then he growled something that sounded suspiciously like a curse on all women and walked away.

Riley whistled for the dogs but didn't follow, making instead for the old lighthouse where she sat down and rested her back against the solid concrete wall, pleased to have something tangible in her life.

CHAPTER TEN

SOMEHOW Mitch made it through the day. A second sleep-less night had left him drained and edgy, so much so he'd snapped at Olivia and brought a storm of tears from the little girl who had already been distressed at leaving her temporary home.

'I want to stay with Riley!' she'd told her father, and he, who'd had similar thoughts at times during the long night, hadn't quite known how to appease her.

Talk of the party had helped, but that had made him think of Riley also. Would she come?

After what had happened, he couldn't blame her if she didn't. Not that she'd seemed the slightest bit affected by the kiss. Taunting him like that afterwards!

His sense of aggravation had returned so, when Olivia had insisted on loading a menagerie of stuffed toy animals into the car before they left the Dennisons for the drive to pre-school—'Riley told me I could have them!'—it had been all he could do not to lose his temper and snap again.

By four-thirty he was ready to take an early mark and go home. To his own home!

Clare reminded him of the meeting.

'Hugh and Frances will both be here to meet Peter's successor, also Tracey and Jill, but Harry's up at the hospital. Mrs Fraser's baby's on the way. He'll be back if it arrives, but probably won't make it.'

She hesitated, and Mitch sensed a wariness in his usually forthright secretary.

'Do you want me to sit in? To take notes or anything?'

Her tone suggested she'd rather be anywhere but present at the meeting, and he couldn't blame her.

'I guess we'll manage,' he said. 'It's not as if it's an interview. Besides, the bus is dropping Olivia here. Could you keep an eye on her?'

Clare's relief was puzzlingly apparent.

Why?

Mitch explored a little further.

'As you're one of the few real "locals" in the building, perhaps you know this person. Susan, isn't it? Didn't Peter say she was from this area?'

'Yes, he did, and, yes I do, which is why I don't want anything to do with the interview,' Clare said bluntly, then she added, 'And not telling you wasn't my idea either.'

She walked away, heading, Mitch guessed, for the washroom, where he couldn't follow to demand an explanation of the cryptic comment.

The explanation became apparent a little later. His tenants were all seated in the lounge room they used as a retreat and meeting place, casually discussing both the worth of having a child psychologist continuing to work from the building and their social engagements for the weekend.

Ribbing him about the party.

Mitch was sitting with his back to the door, and thinking how long it had been since he'd had a social engagement to discuss, when the sight of Hugh rising to his feet told him Susan had arrived.

Clare mumbled what Mitch assumed was 'Susan Barker' by way of introduction, then her tapping footsteps suggested she'd beaten a hasty retreat.

Mitch stood and turned, then felt his jaw drop. Well, it would have dropped if the collar hadn't held it up.

You're an impostor! he wanted to yell, but one look from eyes as cool and grey as ice today made him clamp his lips shut. He watched as she introduced herself to each person in turn, shaking hands and repeating their names and what they did as if to imprint it in her mind.

Imprinting itself in *his* mind was the image in front of him. A slim, elegant figure, her red hair confined in a complicated braid that somehow emphasised the fine bones in her face and drew attention to delicately pink and glossy lips.

'It's my official name,' she murmured as she reached him, holding out her hand as she had to the others, while her eyes challenged him to make a fuss. 'And, yes, I should have told you, but I really wanted to continue working out of the same rooms as Peter. For the clients' sake. I didn't want you having preconceived ideas.'

He shouldn't have kissed her. That was his first thought.

A disastrous one, as it drew his attention and his eyes to her lips and his body began behaving badly.

He wanted to protest—to yell at her for her deception if nothing else—but the cool control in her eyes held him silent. He contented himself with a frown, then nodded to a vacant chair. He'd go along with this nonsense but he didn't have to like it.

He sat down himself and waited—until the silence told him the others must be waiting for him to make a move, deferring to him as landlord.

'You've all seen Susan's CV. You know she's taking over Peter's patients so it makes sense she works from here, but as we've always discussed tenancies before anyone came in, I wanted you to meet her,' he said. 'Who wants to ask questions? Hugh?'

Mitch realised he'd made a tactical error when he saw Frances's frowning reaction. She'd take it as a male thing that he'd asked the only other man present to begin.

He hid a sigh and wondered what the office equivalent of a wife was. He needed one of them, too. Though think ing of the need reminded him of the kiss. Something he didn't want to remember right now.

Naturally, when Frances did break in with her a question of her own, it was sharper than it need have been, but Susan-Riley handled it with tact and, Mitch had to admit, a certain amount of charm. Something that had been singularly lacking in her dealings with him.

The two therapists had their turn, wanting to know what the interviewee had done in the way of teamwork—was she experienced in a team approach to case management and willing to continue to be part of their team on cases?

Mitch winced. He hated to hear patients referred to as 'cases', though he knew the word was used widely in both medicine and the related therapies.

'I don't like to use the word "case",' Susan-Riley said quietly. 'I can't see why we don't talk about client management, or patient management. After all, the "case" really refers to the problem, not the patient, and labelling a patient that way brings with it the negative connotations of the "problem".'

If anyone else had said it, Mitch would have given a small cheer, but to hear the words coming out of that particular mouth, kissable though it might be, only made him suspicious. Had Peter told his former co-worker how Mitch felt, or had Clare been feeding the woman information?

And he'd deal with *her* later!

Tracey was protesting that 'case' was simply a word used by them in private discussions, but Riley countered that such a practice made the word doubly dangerous as it dehumanised the patient at a time when he or she should have been to the forefront of the professional's mind.

Mitch guessed there'd be at least one vote against the letting of the rooms—from Tracey, who was already peevish over being refused the larger space.

'A lot of your experience seems to have been with cancer

patients. We don't have much need for that as kids from here go to the city for treatment.'

'It's not all I do,' Riley replied. 'Although I was involved in that way most recently.'

She spoke firmly, and didn't offer more than was necessary, but Mitch sensed an underlying reserve at odds with the woman he'd met in her other incarnation.

Not that he knew that much about Riley.

Frances asked another question, but his thoughts had been sidetracked.

Not as a person. Barely as a builder.

Which she apparently wasn't!

So why did he feel as if he did know her?

Riley continued to field the questions, but Mitch's silence, his refusal to get involved in any way in this interview process, told her it was all pointless. There was no way he, as senior partner of the loosely formed group, was going to approve her involvement, neither, as owner of the building, was he likely to want to rent the rooms to her.

'I think guidance officers within schools are better suited to provide careers counselling,' she said, in reply to a weakness Frances apparently saw in her experience. 'I can run the aptitude tests and read off results to indicate where a young person's talents might lie, but with the range of career choices available to people these days it's a very specialised field, and the guidance officers have so much more information at their fingertips.'

She slid a glance towards Mitch, who was leaning back in his chair, lowered eyelids hiding his eyes. He could have been asleep for all the notice he was taking of her ordeal.

Frances asked something else, and Riley answered automatically, although her temper, usually under rigid control these days, was rising dangerously.

'Yes, I think counselling has a big part to play in children's adjustment to any ongoing therapy regimes,' she told

Jill in response to a question about a child with cystic fibrosis. 'Though I believe it should be available for the child to use rather than forced onto the child as part of a "management plan".'

She wiggled her fingers in the air to give the words inverted commas and saw Mitch's head tilt forward. Then, to her surprise, he straightened in his chair, looked around the room and said, 'Well, I think that's enough for now.'

And as the others began to gather up their books and papers, he nodded towards Riley.

'I'd like you to stay, please, Susan,' he said, putting special emphasis on the name she'd been christened but had never used.

She closed her eyes, telling herself she would handle the bad news with dignity, not rage.

Definitely not rage, she warned the still simmering anger.

'So, what did you think of them?'

The question was so bizarre she opened her eyes and stared blankly at the man who'd asked it.

'If you take the rooms here, you have to be able to work with the other people in the building,' he said, speaking as if this explanation was all she needed. 'It's important to know what your first impressions are.'

'If I take the rooms!' she scoffed. 'As if you have any intention of letting that happen.'

His eyes narrowed.

'I might!' he said. 'Just answer the question.'

The lid Riley had clamped on her temper lifted.

'I'll answer the question,' she snorted. 'Every person in this room had their own personal agenda, which, in fact, makes me wonder how well you work as a team. Hugh enjoys being a man in a mostly female environment, and taking into account that it's usually a woman who takes the child to the doctor, he's doubly blessed by feminine gratitude and praise.'

Mitch hid a wince as this acute observation made him wonder how she summed him up.

'You, of course—' she didn't leave him wondering long '—are so caught up in your own misery, you quite enjoy the little battles going on within your empire. I imagine if you'd told Frances and Hugh to get their acts together and behave like adults, all the bickering between them would have stopped ages ago.'

Mitch was so incensed that he didn't know which bit to argue first. He opted for attack.

'And what about your own behaviour?' he demanded. 'Not only lying by omission, but using Clare or Peter as a source of information.' He shot her a triumphant look before adding, 'How else would you know Frances and Hugh were at each other's throats?'

Riley's reaction surprised—and mocked—him. She raised her eyebrows and rolled her eyes, and held out her hands in an 'oh, please' gesture!

'I've sat through an hour in their company, remember!' she said. 'If I'd been too insensitive to feel the animosity, I'd have had to have been dead to miss the barbs flying back and forth. And if you really want a run-down of the rest of them, then I'd say Tracey is furious you're even considering leasing the rooms to me, though why she should feel so threatened I have no idea. I'm sure my arguing about the use of the word "case" wasn't the sole reason she was offside.'

Mitch hoped he'd hidden his surprise.

'And Jill—no rash assumptions you'd like to make about her?'

Riley's eyes all but darted fire at him, then she straightened, and in haughty tones said, 'How a man as dense as you will ever find a wife is beyond me. You've been asking me to tell you where to go to meet single women whe you've one who's already in love with you right beneath your nose.'

She paused, but before he could question her about such a wild guess she went on, 'And getting back to your "lying by omission" accusation, would you have considered leasing me the rooms if I'd told you I was the candidate?'

She had him there, but the statement about Jill was still rankling.

And bothering him, for he was fond of the quiet, hardworking physio, but he'd certainly never considered her in a—well, wifely way.

'What makes you say that about Jill?'

To his surprise, Riley blushed, and for the first time since she'd stridden into the room and caused further chaos in his life, she looked uncertain.

'Forget I said that,' she told him. 'That wasn't fair. It was an impression—nothing more.'

But there was more, he was certain, although he knew for sure Riley Dennison had no intention of telling him.

Which reminded him—

'And what's this Susan Barker business?' he demanded. 'Do you always use an alias? And if you're a psychologist, what the hell were you doing, pretending to supervise the building job at my house?'

His visitor sighed and he noticed there were shadows beneath her eyes.

And was vindictive enough to hope she, too, might have suffered a sleepless night. Then the pale eyes met his and he forgot about vindication as he fought for breath.

'I've been on jobs with my father all my life,' she said. 'The men called me little Riley and the name stuck. Even at school, only teachers ever called me Susan, and usually not for long.'

He had a vivid image of the little redheaded child scrambling around building sites behind her father, and knew instinctively that Riley had done a good job with his daughter.

Better than he, Mitch, was doing with his at the moment!

She was still talking, explaining, something about someone called Jack.

'We'd paired off at school, friends first then boyfriend and girlfriend, so when he decided he wanted to be a builder and became apprenticed to Dad, I thought that's what I wanted as well.'

Mitch waited, aware this conversation was important to him, although he didn't know why.

'Dad was loving, but he was strict with me, and Jack, working for him, was afraid of doing the wrong thing so we got married.'

'Girlfriend and boyfriend? You're saying you got married so you could have sex?'

The cool eyes grew hot with wrath.

'You don't have to make it sound like an aberration,' she snapped. 'We were young, our hormones were leaping around all over the place, we fancied each other like mad so, yes, we got married to have sex.'

'And didn't you enjoy it?'

It seemed the logical question to ask but judging from the flush on Riley's cheeks her temper was rising, not falling.

'Of course I enjoyed it!' she said. 'Why wouldn't I?'

Mitch felt slightly put out by this declaration, but he rallied.

'Well, apparently you're not still married.' A dreadful thought struck him and his own anger shimmied back to life. 'Or is Jack still in Sydney? Have you been kissing me on the headland while all the while you had a husband stashed away somewhere?'

She swept to her feet and took a quick turn around the room.

'You make it sound as if I've been making a habit of kissing you!' she stormed, throwing out her arms to emphasise the absurdity of the statement. 'And for your information, Jack is not stashed in Sydney. He's alive and well and living in Port Anderson, and as the doctor doesn't want Dad working for a while he'll be taking over your extension on Monday!'

Mitch wanted to object to having Riley's ex-husband anywhere near his house, but couldn't think of a reasonable argument to back up the protest so attacked from another angle instead.

'If you enjoyed the sex, why didn't you stay married?' he demanded, then heard an echo of the words and knew he'd left himself wide open.

'This from a man who's looking for a wife because he can't run his own life? Of course, you wouldn't understand.' She stopped pacing and stood in front of him, magnificent in her fury. 'I happen to think there's more to marriage than good sex. Or that there should be. Jack and I liked each other, we were friends, but that was it.'

She eyed him fiercely, as if daring him to take her lightly, and added, 'I realised I wanted more. I still want more. I want love, Dr Hammond. A pulse that trips when I'm with that special man. A heat that's more than need. A oneness with another person that's more a communion of souls than a tangible entity. I didn't find that with Jack and rather than cheat both of us of the opportunity of maybe finding it one day I left. And because I'd made such a hash of my own young life, I decided to learn how to help other kids.'

'You became a child psychologist,' Mitch said, his mind racing through a thousand random thoughts. Statistics. Children who lost a parent often married young or had a child out of wedlock—someone special for them to love.

Riley was pacing again.

Would he have to guard against it with Olivia?

Could sex with Jack have been *that* good? Didn't it get better with age? How old had they been? How old when she'd left?

Thinking about anything and everything.

Everything but Riley's definition of love.

He didn't want to think about that.

Thought of Mrs Martin instead.

'I've a patient I'd like you to see fairly urgently,' he said.

Riley stopped pacing so suddenly she all but overbalanced. Steadying herself against the back of a chair, she stared at the man who'd turned her world upside down.

'Are you saying you'll actually refer to me?'

He frowned at her.

'Of course I'll refer to you. Your references are excellent, and Peter says you know what you're doing. Mrs Martin. She's not a teenage pregnancy—'

Riley held up her hand and interrupted him. 'Hang on a minute. Let's get this straight. Do I get the rooms?'

'Of course you get the rooms!' Mitch said crossly, waving his hand as if it was a minor consideration and totally unimportant.

'There's no "of course" about it!' Riley told him. 'You're the most irrational man I've ever met. Quixotic. Look at you. Neck in a brace because you tried to catch a falling body. And as for this wife business...' She threw up her arms in supplication. 'Maybe the gods understand you, but a mere mortal sure has difficulties.'

Mitch stared at her in disbelief. She was describing so accurately how he felt about her. A total lack of comprehension akin to bewilderment. As if the parameters of normality had been shifted so far he could no longer find them!

Best if he stuck to practical matters.

'Will you see Mrs Martin?' he demanded.

'When?' Riley countered. 'Is it urgent enough for you to want me to speak to her today, or would Monday do?'

Well, at least that worked, Mitch thought.

'Monday will be fine, but if you can give me a time I'll phone and tell her. It might save her some heart-searching over the weekend.'

'Heart-searching?'

She said the word so softly that Mitch wondered if it meant something personal to her. She slipped into the chair opposite him and said, 'Perhaps you'd better explain.'

He found himself telling her not only about Mrs Martin, but about the pain he felt for her, being forced into a decision she didn't want to make. Then Blythe came into the conversation and he explained her predicament, finally relaxing enough under the influence of shop-talk to smile at Riley and say, 'I'm glad you're here. We need you.'

She almost smiled back then murmured something about checking an appointment time and left the room.

He watched the door close and decided he should also tell her he'd knocked the ladder out from under her and hadn't so much caught her as grabbed at her to save both of them from disaster. But while that might make him look less quixotic, it hardly painted him in a good light.

Especially after he'd blackmailed her with his supposed 'good deed'.

He scratched his neck inside the collar. A week was nearly up. It was coming off tomorrow.

Tomorrow! The party. Would Riley come?

She poked her head back into the room at that moment. 'Tell Mrs Martin ten o'clock on Monday, and if that doesn't suit, then twelve—that's Peter's lunch-hour so there won't be any patients.'

And before he realised it she was gone, whisking away with the air of a woman who had far better things to do than chat to him.

Mitch checked the time, realised how late it was and hurried out to the reception area where Olivia was patiently drawing fish and colouring them in while Clare did some filing.

'Thanks, Clare,' he said, as he lifted his daughter into his arms and gave her a hug and kiss. 'That went on longer than I thought.'

'Who's going to build our stensions if Riley comes to work here?' Olivia demanded.

'Someone called Jack Barker, apparently,' Mitch answered, and watched colour creep into his secretary's cheeks. 'And well you may blush, Clare!' he added. 'You've some explaining to do.'

She pushed some papers across the desk towards him.

'Maybe!' she admitted. 'But right now this is more important. These are the salads I've ordered—they'll be delivered mid-afternoon tomorrow. Rob will drop the meat off for you about then as well.'

Mitch nodded, grateful Clare had taken control of the party arrangements and had a brother who was a butcher.

'He'll pick up bread rolls from the baker next door and bring them at the same time, and I've asked Riley to come along and give me a hand setting up.'

Before he could object, Olivia crowed with delight that Riley would be early, and when he did manage to make a point his secretary waved away his protests.

'All men think a barbecue is simply a matter of tossing steaks over the coals. There's a lot more to it than that, but we'll cope. I've left it for you to organise the drinks.'

Mitch gave up. He might not relish the idea of seeing more of Riley than absolutely necessary, but there was no way he was going to win an argument with Clare.

He gathered up Olivia's belongings and slipped her artwork into a folder to take home, then escorted his daughter out to the car. Driving back to his own home was a relief, he told himself, and when he opened the door he almost believed it.

'Oh, Daddy, isn't it pretty!' Olivia exclaimed, and while, out loud, he agreed, privately he thought it was beautiful.

And homely somehow!

Great baskets of greenery, eucalyptus and pine from the perfume, had been placed against newly restored and painted walls. Smaller bowls of similarly exuberant foliage were dotted around on tables and sideboards.

'Let's see your bathroom,' Olivia suggested, and he followed her through to a pristine bedroom, though still with her small bed against the wall.

In the bathroom, new tiles gleamed and a faint musky smell of air freshener almost took away the smell of paint.

While Olivia darted off to get her stuffed animal friends from the car, Mitch meandered back through the house—feeling the warmth of home again—and finally, drawn by a different aroma, reached the kitchen.

'Welcome home,' the note said, but it was the oven and the casserole nestling inside it that drew his attention.

'The kitchen smells like Riley's,' Olivia announced, coming to join him a minute later. 'Is she here?'

He saw the excitement in his daughter's eyes as she glanced around, perhaps expecting Riley to be hiding nearby.

'No, she's not here,' Mitch said gently, and the disappointment in Olivia's eyes made him ache for her.

'I wish she was,' Olivia sighed.

Which was when the thought occurred to him. He wanted a wife—who better than Riley, who already knew and seemed to like Olivia?

And Olivia liked her.

She could cook, and was darned efficient, which was really what he needed.

Then he remembered what she'd said about her previous marriage. About wanting love. An emotion he was reasonably sure didn't exist—or, if it did, rarely survived.

'I'd be offering her false coin,' he said aloud, and by the time he'd explained the meaning of the phrase to Olivia, he'd put such rash thoughts out of his mind and kept them out by writing a list of drinks he'd need for the party.

CHAPTER ELEVEN

SHEER exhaustion ensured Mitch slept well, and when Olivia woke him the next morning, he felt fit and ready to face whatever the day would throw at him.

First, he'd take off the collar.

With his daughter's help he cleaned the barbecue, hosed the paved area then set chairs and tables around beneath the trees in the back yard.

Olivia plucked hibiscus from the bushes and placed them on the tables, and the festive look started a faint ripple of excitement.

'Come on, we'll go shopping,' he said, when the yard was ready. He took her hand and off they went, returning suitably laden an hour later. He set the drinks into the cool boxes then spilled ice around them, and was stacking more ice in the freezer when the doorbell rang.

'The visitors are early,' Olivia declared, racing to open the door.

Mitch followed more slowly, in time to see a tall, well-built, handsome stranger standing on his porch.

'Can I help you?' he asked.

'I'm Jack Barker,' the man said, stepping forward with his hand outstretched.

Mitch forced himself to behave with civility, although extending his own hand was an effort and the polite greeting came out through clenched teeth.

'I thought I'd better introduce myself,' Jack added, 'and take a look at what's what. Riley's given me the plans.'

He waved the sheaf of paper at Mitch who stepped back far enough to allow the man to enter.

Somehow he managed to explain what was to be done, to point out the small bedroom where the stairs would go and assure Jack the electricity had been turned off to that end of the house.

He was wondering if the chap would ever leave when another car pulled up outside and Olivia's glad cry of greeting told him he was about to see a meeting of the exes!

And if he'd hoped for reserve or constraint he was doomed to disappointment.

'Jack's here?' he heard Riley say in tones of such gladness he wanted to send her away.

But she was already dancing down his hall, then flinging herself into the man's arms. And Jack wasn't behaving any better, lifting her off the ground and twirling her in the air.

'So how's my first best girl?' Jack asked, after he'd set her on her feet and planted a kiss on her lips.

Riley positively glowed at him while Mitch felt a glower coming on.

'First best when you've what? Three other best girls now?'

'Three and a half,' Jack said, at which stage Clare, who'd apparently followed Riley into the house, grabbed Mitch by the arm and steered him towards the kitchen.

'Standing there glaring at them isn't doing any good!' she said to him.

'Did you see the way he kissed her?' Mitch fumed, shaking off Clare's restraining hand and peering back towards the hall.

'She's an old friend from for ever, as well as his ex-wife,' Clare told him. 'And anyway, why should it matter to you how he kisses her?'

That stumped him and he opened the freezer again and looked at the ice. He didn't need to look at the ice but it gave him something to do and the cool air was beneficial.

Fortunately for his sanity, Rob arrived, and by the time

he'd sorted out the meat and finished the Clare-appointed task of buttering bread rolls it was time to have a shower and change.

And if working beside Riley in his own kitchen had affected him, he hoped she hadn't noticed. It was thinking about the wife thing that had done it, he decided. Made it all seem possible somehow, in spite of her preoccupation with the 'L' word.

The party went off well—so well no one wanted to go home. At ten Riley took an exhausted Olivia to bed, and sang to her until she went to sleep. An hour later she was considering making an escape herself when Mitch, who was rostered on for the weekend emergencies, was called out to one of Harry's patients who had gone into early labour.

'I can take Olivia home with me,' Clare offered. She and Riley were in the kitchen, washing up.

'I don't know about that,' Riley said. 'She was so tired. Being woken and shifted might really upset her.' She dithered for a moment, then suggested reluctantly, 'I suppose I could stay the night.'

She didn't look at Mitch as she said it, but he'd been so politely cool to her all evening she knew he'd consider the offer nothing more than it was—an offer of help.

'You don't have to do that!' he protested.

'I know I don't have to,' Riley retorted. 'But I'm offering!'

She dared him to refuse, but he wasn't going to give in easily.

'I can't imagine why I didn't think of this happening and keep Gary for the night!' he complained, and this time Clare responded.

'Because the woman isn't due for three weeks, that's probably why. You and Harry discussed it and decided it was so unlikely anyone would be needed this weekend that you might as well take the roster. But in the meantime are you going to stand here arguing while she gives birth on her own, or are you going to say ''thank you kindly'' to Riley and accept her offer?'

Mitch frowned at his secretary.

'Boy, are you tetchy!' he muttered, then he turned and looked at Riley. She saw the doubt in his eyes, and read something else in them she didn't understand, for it looked like despair.

'Thank you kindly,' he said, then he turned away.

She watched him go, wanting nothing more than to follow, to take him in her arms, to hold him close and tell him everything would be all right. That she was there and he needn't worry.

'I must be going soft in my old age,' she muttered, grabbing another pile of dirty plates, plunging them into the soapy water and scrubbing at them as if her life depended on it.

The final guest departed and Riley walked around the back yard, collecting glasses and the dirty plates that had escaped the trawl she and Clare had done earlier. Tiredness dogged her steps and, realising she'd be likely to break something if she started another lot of washing-up, she stacked them on the kitchen bench.

Mitch could do them in the morning.

On that thought she checked Olivia then headed into the darkness at the far end of the house, wanting only to crawl into bed. Using the dim illumination of moonlight through the window, she stripped off and, not having any nightclothes with her, crawled naked into Mrs Rush's bed.

What if Olivia wakes?

I won't hear her from here.

She'll see her father's empty bed and go looking for him

Would she think to look in here?

Riley thought back to her childhood. She'd been reasonably brave but there had been no way she'd have walked down that dark corridor.

Perhaps she won't wake...

But if she does...

With a groan of frustration, Riley sat up. Then she dragged the top sheet free of the blankets and wrapped it securely around her body.

Thus clad, she padded back down the dark corridor. She'd share Olivia's bed. Reassure the child with her presence.

Seeing Olivia askew across the bed put paid to that idea, but Mitch's bed was there—and wide enough for half a dozen if they all lay on their sides. If she stayed on the very edge, near Olivia...

Still wrapped in the sheet, she eased into the bed, curled up on the edge and, in spite of fearing sleep would never come, promptly fell asleep.

A loud ringing noise woke her, shrilling into her ears with a terrible persistence. She pulled a pillow over her head but the noise continued, then the scuffle of Olivia's feet on the carpet reminded her of where she was and she bolted out of the bed, tripped over a trailing bit of sheet and had to stop and re-wrap herself before proceeding any further.

She made it to the front door as Mitch, clad in a pair of lurid boxer shorts, appeared from the direction of the other bedroom and opened it.

The noise continued, and in a replay of another meeting Mitch tried to reef the mechanism off the wall.

'I thought someone was going to fix this!' he growled, but Riley was already seeking the power point so she could stop the noise.

'It's in the kitchen. I'll turn it off,' Olivia offered, and she darted away.

Mitch, meanwhile, had turned to greet the woman who'd started the noise.

'Come in, Mrs Marshall. Excuse me while I get some clothes on. Late call, I've not long been in. Baby boy, but he took his time coming into the world.'

He stumbled out the words and Riley guessed he'd answered the door without realising how little he was wearing, and was now scurrying for cover. But as he passed her his stride faltered, and his gaze raked over her. Then he shook his head as if to clear it, and continued on towards his bedroom.

'Riley Dennison! What are you doing here? And dressed like that? What's going on here? What kind of place is this? Mr Marshall wouldn't like me to be mixed up in any funny business.' Mrs Marshall had indeed come in.

She was standing in front of Riley, blocking any hope of escape.

Reduced to six-year-old status, when Mrs Marshall had been her Sunday school teacher, Riley stuttered and stammered and failed to come up with an understandable explanation.

'I can't understand your father allowing something like this!' Mrs Marshall continued. 'No one cares about city ways in the city, where fornication might be all the go, but here—'

'Fornication?' Riley repeated the word in disbelief, then, realising how things must look to Mrs Marshall, she tried again to explain, but Mrs Marshall was in full flight, bringing down on Riley's head all manner of doom and damnation.

Mitch returned, this time clad in jeans and a loose sweater, but his feet were bare. They looked so pale and sexy somehow that Riley's attention was diverted from the tirade.

'And as for you, Doctor. What would your patients think?'

To Riley's relief, Mrs Marshall turned her attack on Mitch.

'About what?' Mitch said, and Riley heard the bewilderment in his voice and started to smile.

'Fornication,' she said helpfully.

Mrs Marshall glared at her.

'That's what it is, my girl, and don't you joke about it. Especially not with an innocent child in the house.'

Riley choked back a giggle, brought on mainly by the look on Mitch's face. She wondered briefly where the innocent child might be, but all thought of Olivia and all desire to laugh fled when, a second later, Mitch put his arm around Riley's shoulders, tucked her up against his body and turned to the infuriated woman.

'I think you've got it all wrong, Mrs Marshall,' he said in a dangerously calm voice. 'Miss Dennison happens to be my fiancée, and she was forced to stay last night because I was called out and I couldn't leave Olivia alone.'

'Oh, really!' Mrs Marshall said, making the words a statement of disbelief. Then she turned around and sailed majestically out of the house.

'Well, that went well!' Mitch muttered, his arm still around Riley's bare shoulders.

'It was the fornication that did it!' she said, laughter bubbling up again.

'As if!' Mitch muttered.

He sounded almost desperate, and Riley eased away so she could turn and look into his face.

'What's wrong?'

He shrugged.

'That was my temporary housekeeper.'

He nodded towards the door.

'Mrs Marshall? She was here for an interview? I thought

she must have been collecting for the church, or some other good cause.'

'She'd already had the interview—and I'd accepted her. She was here to meet Olivia—for Olivia to meet her.'

'Well, it's a good thing she's gone,' Riley told him. 'She'd have been a terrible influence on the little one. I've barely got over the harm she did me when I was six.'

'That's all very well,' Mitch growled. 'But at least she was someone!' He looked at Riley, his eyes so intent she felt her skin grow hot.

'If you'd go and put some clothes on I might be able to think,' he added, and she needed no further prompting.

She fled.

Mitch watched her disappear down the corridor. His body was behaving badly again—this time reacting to a sleep-ruffled, sheet-wrapped Riley.

He wandered through to the kitchen where Olivia, trained to a new independence by the Dennisons, was eating her breakfast.

'Did that scary lady go away?' she asked, and Mitch nodded, then considered the adjective.

'What made you think she was scary?'

'She yelled at Riley and made Riley look sad.'

The anger that had prompted him to defend the woman who'd caused so much havoc in his life stirred again.

'Well, she's gone. Mrs Marshall, not Riley.'

'Riley's gone, too—or going,' a soft voice said. 'I'm on my way. Just came to say goodbye to my favourite four-year-old. Do I get a kiss?'

She flashed into the kitchen like a sudden surge of wind, flung words here and there, caught Olivia's flying form and kissed her soundly on the cheek, then set her back on her stool and with a waggle of her fingers headed out again.

'Wait!' Mitch said, and dashed after her, catching her as she left the family room.

'I really must go,' she said, moving backwards as she spoke. 'Dad will be worried.'

He knew it must be at least part-lie because her usually candid gaze failed to meet his.

'Riley—' he began, but she forestalled him, raising those lovely eyes, blue-green this morning, and finally looking directly at him.

'I realise I've blown your child-minding arrangements, but Dad has to take it easy for a while so he won't be working. I know he'll be happy to take care of Olivia in the afternoons and he's a better cook than I am, so doing something about dinner for the pair of you won't bother him.'

She hesitated, then added, 'I'll get him to phone you to talk about bus times and practical matters.' And with a final 'I guess I'll see you Monday' she whisked out of the house.

But not out of his life, he reminded himself as depression threatened to descend.

No way! The more he thought about it, the more convinced he was that Riley would make a perfect wife.

Well, maybe not perfect. He smiled to himself as he matched that description to Riley. But life would never be dull!

She might not know it, but she was definitely going to become a permanent fixture around this place.

All he had to do was figure out some way to convince her.

The contact with her father would help.

And having her close at hand at work.

He mulled over ways and means while he cleaned up the last reminders of the party, then took Olivia to the park and thought some more.

It wasn't until Monday that Mitch realised the one thing he hadn't taken into consideration in his plot to win Riley for his wife was the size of the town.

Just as his patients the previous week had demanded to hear the story of his trendy new haircut, by Monday the topic on all the women's lips was his engagement.

'You've got to put a stop to this,' the other party to the betrothal said, storming into his office at lunchtime.

He decided innocence might work.

'To what? Your tenancy? Half a day on the job and you're not happy?'

She scowled at him and he realised that even Riley's scowls made the day seem brighter—made him feel more alive.

'T-to this engagement nonsense!' she said, positively stuttering with rage.

It turned her cheeks pink and made her eyes sparkle, and he was thinking how magnificent she looked when she added, 'People are giving me presents!'

'Presents?' He really should stop thinking about flashing eyes and get with it here. 'What do you mean, presents?'

Her scowl deepened and he noticed how dark her eyebrows looked against her pale skin.

'Little gifts wrapped in pretty paper—that kind of present, stupid,' the woman he hoped to make his wife said. 'Teatowel and apron-type presents!'

'Really?' The idea fascinated him. Did that kind of thing still go on? Of course, Riley was a local, known to a lot of people in the town.

A slight niggle of conscience stabbed briefly as he considered the implications of this. Given this reaction, was it fair to her to keep up the pretence?

But it wasn't a pretence—at least, he didn't want it to be...

'Well? Aren't you going to say something? Are you just

going to sit there looking pleased with yourself and smiling secret smiles while my life races towards disaster?'

Secret smiles indeed. He gave her a real smile and said, 'Would it be such a disaster? Being engaged, even married, to me?'

She looked at him for a long, long time, during which his intestines knotted and his intercostal muscles seized up, making it difficult to breathe.

Then she said, 'I think so.' Her voice was so soft he barely heard it. She turned away, walking out the door before he could find the words to stop her.

Riley started back towards the office she was sharing with Peter for this week, then, realising she didn't want to talk to anyone, swung about and headed out the front door of the building.

She'd gone in to talk to Mitch about Mrs Martin, and walked out so confused she wondered if she'd ever be able to concentrate on a patient again.

Given the male tendency to think in straight lines, Mitch had linked his foolish and impulsive defence of her—telling Mrs Marshall she was his fiancée—with his new determination to find a wife. He'd added two and two and come up with her—Riley Dennison.

So easy—from *his* point of view!

And while she was reluctantly coming to realise that she'd fallen headlong in love with the man, so that it would be the pinnacle of all her dreams to marry Mitch, she still had this hang-up about love.

About giving and receiving love—being loved back!

She walked to the river-mouth and watched the tide surging in, then, accepting that the river wasn't going to solve her problem, turned and walked back again.

'Could you tell Mitch I need to talk to him about Mrs Martin?' She poked her head into his suite of rooms to give the message to Clare.

Clare beckoned her to come in, but the last thing Riley wanted was a heart to heart with Mitch's secretary. In fact, the less contact she had with anyone from those rooms, the better.

Mitch came at five, when Peter had departed and she was reading through files, trying to absorb the background information of the next day's patients.

'I've spoken to your father and told him I might be late. Do you want to go somewhere for a drink? We could just as easily talk about Mrs Martin in relaxed surroundings.'

Riley knew exactly how her body would behave in more relaxed surroundings and vetoed the idea.

'I think work should be discussed at work,' she said primly. 'Mrs Martin. Did she tell you who the father was? Why she's so upset and confused?'

Mitch shook his head, but as he slid into a chair across the desk from her the concern in his eyes told her he'd accepted this was nothing more than a patient-related discussion.

'He's a well-known local identity in their town. Ten years older than Mrs Martin, and with a grown family—two daughters in their twenties.'

'I can hear worse coming. I vaguely recall her mentioning the words "married man" at our first meeting,' Mitch said, and Riley nodded.

'Married and nursing his wife who's been an invalid for years. She has Alzheimer's and, although she was OK at first, she's now deteriorated to the stage where she needs full-time care. He gave up his job to do it, and Mrs Martin, after her husband died, used to go and sit with the woman to give him a break.'

'And started an affair.'

Riley looked at the man who sat across the desk. She'd talked to him about love once before and had sensed his withdrawal, but right now she felt it was important he accept its existence. For only then could he understand his patient's plight.

'They fell in love,' she said, 'which I think is very different. An affair you can get over. An affair isn't going anywhere—it's a temporary thing. These two people feel very deeply about each other.'

She hesitated, drew a deep breath, then went on, 'To the extent that Mrs Martin, who has always longed for a child and feels this pregnancy is like a gift from God, will probably opt for termination, rather than see the man she loves, or his family, hurt by the gossip which could result from her keeping the child.'

'But if she wants the child so badly—' Mitch began.

'It's for his sake she'd make the decision,' Riley interrupted. 'So he won't be hurt. She knows how people will react towards to him if they learn he's been cheating on his wife. And what about his daughters? How will they feel towards him when they hear about it? These are the things tormenting Mrs Martin. I can understand why termination seems a logical solution.'

'But surely she shouldn't make a decision for his sake without consulting him,' Mitch said. 'He might feel equally strongly—he might want the child. Can you advise someone to make a choice like that without consulting the father?'

Riley shrugged.

'I can't advise anyone to do anything,' she explained. 'I can only listen and help people work out what they want for themselves.'

'But she could leave town—have the child somewhere else. Surely if she wants a child, that's the answer?'

'And walk away from the man she loves when he needs the support and comfort only she can give him? That's not how love works.'

Riley heard an echo of the words in her head. Mitch needed her. Well, he needed a wife.

Looked at this way, was being loved in return really so important?

'Has she decided?'

The question brought her mind back to where it should have been.

'No, not yet. She told me she has an appointment to see you later in the week and will call in to see me at the same time.'

Mitch nodded, then he sighed.

'I hate this part of the job,' he muttered, then he scowled at her. 'That love stuff you talk about has a lot to answer for!'

The phrase returned to haunt Mitch later that night as he tossed and turned in bed. Every time he closed his eyes he had an image of his hands unwrapping Riley from the sheet. Untwining it carefully as one would handle a very special present.

Then the word 'present' would give rise to images of Riley in an apron—just an apron—and he'd open his eyes and stare at the ceiling again.

Perhaps if he went back to square one—to the wife-hunt…

But if half the town thought he was engaged, he could hardly start dating other women.

No, marrying Riley seemed like the best idea. All he had to do was convince her.

CHAPTER TWELVE

'WE'VE only known each other a week,' Riley pointed out, when Mitch put the marriage notion to her the next day.

'We can get to know each other better,' he argued. 'What are you doing tonight?'

'Running a "say no to drugs" class at the high school,' she said. 'And that should be enough to convince you I'm not the wife you need. I'll be doing a lot of evening courses and classes, so I won't be there to cook your dinner or look after Olivia for you.'

'But we'll have Mrs Rush,' Mitch reminded her. 'She'll be back eventually. Or, once we're organised and the extensions are done, we could make other housekeeper-type arrangements if you don't want someone living in.'

'Like Mrs Marshall?' Riley said dryly, and, realising he'd lost the round, Mitch retreated.

He tried again the following week. By then, knowing he'd seen Blythe Reid, he had another patient to use as an excuse to see her.

'I've introduced her to Mrs Martin,' Riley told him, when he'd settled into what he was beginning to think of as his chair in her room. 'I thought they might be able to talk things through together.'

Mitch remembered how he'd linked the two in his mind and smiled.

'It can't do any harm. And nor would your coming out to dinner with me. How about it?'

'Why?' Riley demanded, in a voice that didn't bode well for the suggestion.

'It's part of the courtship ritual,' Mitch told her. 'A date.'

'Oh, a date?' she said, mocking him with her startled tone and teasing eyes. 'No thanks.'

'Why not?' he demanded, wondering why on earth he was persisting in his efforts. Well, he knew the answer to that—he wanted her. She haunted his nights and made his days murder as he anticipated yet dreaded seeing her.

What was a bigger worry was how, if she really meant the no she kept on saying, he was going to get over wanting her.

'Because I know your plan. I helped you formulate it, remember. You're looking for a wife and I'm convenient.'

'But don't you like me?' he said, doing the plaintive thing so well he almost felt sorry for himself.

'No!' she said, but he saw the colour in her cheeks and knew it was a lie.

It gave him hope as he retreated yet again.

Riley watched him go and wondered if she was being stupid. The attraction she felt for him was so strong, it had taken a mammoth effort of will to not hurl herself across the desk and into his arms.

And she was missing Olivia as well, the feel of the child in her arms, the chubbiness of her body, and trusting blueness of her eyes.

She tried to concentrate on work, using the task of learning about all Peter's clients to blot out other considerations. Visiting the hospital at the weekend, talking to other children.

Then, a week later, Mrs Martin phoned, and Riley knew she had to share the news with Mitch.

'Is he still here?' she said to Clare who was leaving the rooms as Riley approached.

'You mean the grouch? Yep, he's in there.' She gave Riley a considering look. 'And if you're the reason he's so bad-tempered, then how about you give us all a break and go out with the man?'

Riley shrugged, though she felt guilty that her refusal to fall in with Mitch's plans should be causing trouble for other people.

She tapped on the door of his office then walked in. He was sitting with his back to the desk, his feet on the window-sill, presumably staring out at the blue winter sky.

'I thought you'd gone,' he said, and Riley realised he must think it was Clare who'd entered.

'It's not her, it's me,' she said, not making much sense because the sight of him, and her reaction to it, was absorbing far too much of her attention.

He dropped his feet back to the ground and spun around. 'Oh!'

'Oh' wasn't very encouraging, and seeing the lines of tiredness in his face was making her heart falter, but she held her ground.

'It's about Mrs Martin. She's decided.' And suddenly the memory of the woman's visit came flooding back and Riley had to blink back a sudden wetness in her eyes.

'She's so happy!' she told Mitch, her voice catching on the words. 'She did what you suggested, talked to her lover, but not only to him but to his daughters as well. She told them how much she loved him and how she didn't want to hurt him in any way, and asked for their advice.'

She smiled with remembered joy.

'They all came in to see me together. Mrs Martin and Bill—his name's Bill—and the two daughters—one of them is pregnant, too. It turns out the daughters knew their father had been much happier lately and hoped it was because he had someone special in his life.'

Mitch stood up and came around the desk, settling against it with his long legs crossed at the ankles, his arms folded on his chest.

'So she'll keep the baby?'

Riley, disconcerted by his closeness, nodded, then remembered there was more to tell.

'And they'll all stand by her, show their delight and welcome her into their family, which should defuse the gos-
sips.'

'A very important consideration,' Mitch said gravely,
'given the problems I'm having with my wife-hunt.'

He waited for a moment but there was no way Riley was
going to take the bait.

'So, she's sorted out, but what about Blythe? Doesn't
Mrs Martin finding a solution make her decision harder?'

Riley shook her head.

'That's my second bit of news. Mrs Martin has told
Blythe if she decides to keep her baby she can go and live
with her. That way, when Blythe's baby's born she can go
back to school and Mrs Martin will take care of both babies
when Blythe's not there. She's not pressuring Blythe, just
offering her an option should she decide that way.'

Mitch nodded, but Riley guessed he was no longer thinking about Blythe—or Mrs Martin.

'And now you've sorted out everyone else's problems,
what about mine?' he asked.

Riley shifted uneasily in the chair. She knew where this
conversation was going and tried to head it off.

'Need some pregnancy counselling, do you?' she said
lightly.

He shook his head.

'No, it's worse than that,' he said. 'Should I sit down?'

Riley felt her skin grow taut. This was a new reaction to
Mitch's presence. One she hadn't yet learned to handle.
And now he was moving closer, leaning towards her, as if
to touch—

'Stay right where you are,' she warned him. He leaned
back again, but said nothing, so the silence grew until it
was more than she could bear.

'Well?' she said, and he smiled as if he'd won.

'I don't know where to start,' he complained. 'Don't you offer prompts? Introduce yourself and ask me how you can help?'

'I'll help by walking out if you don't get on with it,' she threatened. 'And if you're just wasting my time, I'll—'

'OK! OK! I get the picture.' He shrugged his broad shoulders, ran his hand over his lengthening hair and shot a rueful smile in Riley's direction.

'It's this love thing,' he said at last. 'It keeps cropping up. I mean, look at Mrs Martin. Makes you wonder.'

Riley's heart was racing, and her stomach had squeezed into a knot, but she forced herself to remain calm—and gave him the prompt.

'Wonder what?'

His eyes smiled down at her.

'If it could exist? And survive? Perhaps even grow?'

'You love Olivia. You must know it exists.'

Now his lips smiled as well.

'Ah, but love for a child—for a family member—that's different.' He cocked his head to one side and looked at her. 'Isn't it?'

'Why should it be?' Riley said, falling easily into the counselling pattern of turning questions back on the questioner. 'Why shouldn't love be all-encompassing? Varied by degrees, of course, and taking different forms, but I don't see it as a pretty concept that comes with a use-by date. Surely it's more like a plant, a living entity, which responds to care and nurturing by growing stronger and more vigorous.'

'And what does it feel like, Riley?' he asked. 'Can you tell me that?'

Riley looked up and saw something in his eyes that unknotted her stomach but caused problems with her lungs.

She tried to breathe but still didn't have sufficient air for speech, so in the end it was Mitch who spoke again.

'Does it come with a big weight of uncertainty that drags at the chest? Does it bring sleepless nights, haunted by visions of a red-haired woman? Does it make a man uncomfortable, and bad-tempered, and totally out of sorts, because he doesn't know how the object of all this emotional turmoil feels about him?'

'You don't believe in love,' Riley reminded him. 'You think marriage would work better as a business arrangement.'

'I *didn't* believe in love,' he told her. 'I thought marriage *might* work better as a business arrangement. Past tense Riley Dennison, and if you don't believe me, I'll show you.'

He swooped towards her and lifted her out of the chair drawing her into his arms then silencing any protest she might have considered making with a hot, demanding kiss

So demanding that Riley found herself giving in to it then making some demands of her own.

Much later, he eased her shaking body back down into the chair.

'Sit there,' he said, and she guessed from the tremor in his voice that he wasn't any more in control than she was 'Phone calls to make.'

It didn't make a lot of sense but she was happy to sit Happy to have a moment to try to piece together what was happening.

Could Mitch really love her?

'It's Mitch, Riley,' she heard him say, and it took her moment to realise he was talking to her father. 'I'm going to be late. Can you stay on until Gary gets there?'

Her father must be saying something, then Mitch smiled and spoke again. 'And while I've got you on the phone, do I have your permission to marry your daughter?'

Riley shot out of the chair and started for the desk, but Mitch held her away from the phone as he listened to her father's reply.

'Love her, sir?' she heard Mitch say, and he grinned at the 'her' in question as he added, 'I guess I must. Why else would I want to marry such a forceful, argumentative, trouble-causing woman?'

He chuckled at something her father must have said, then he hung up and pulled Riley close, folding her against his heart and telling her in other words and other ways just how much he loved her.

MILLS & BOON®

Makes any time special™

Mills & Boon publish 29 new titles every month. Select from...

...ern Romance™   Tender Romance™

M...   Sensual Romance™

...al Romance™   Historical Romance™

MAT2

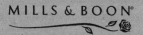

A Perfect Family

An enthralling family saga by bestselling author

PENNY JORDAN

Published 20th July

Available at branches of WH Smith, Tesco, Martins, RS McCall, Forbuoys, Borders, Easons, Sainsbury, Woolworth and most good paperback booksho

4 FREE

books and a surprise gift!

We would like to take this opportunity to thank you for reading this Mills & Boon® book by offering you the chance to take FOUR more specially selected titles from the Medical Romance™ series absolutely FREE! We're also making this offer to introduce you to the benefits of the Reader Service™—

- ★ FREE home delivery
- ★ FREE gifts and competitions
- ★ FREE monthly Newsletter
- ★ Exclusive Reader Service discounts
- ★ Books available before they're in the shops

Accepting these FREE books and gift places you under no obligation to buy, you may cancel at any time, even after receiving your free shipment. Simply complete your details below and return the entire page to the address below. *You don't even need a stamp!*

YES! Please send me 4 free Medical Romance books and a surprise gift. I understand that unless you hear from me, I will receive 6 superb new titles every month for just £2.49 each, postage and packing free. I am under no obligation to purchase any books and may cancel my subscription at any time. The free books and gift will be mine to keep in any case.

M1ZEA

Ms/Mrs/Miss/Mr ....Initials...............................
BLOCK CAPITALS PLEASE

Surname...

Address..

....

....Postcode...................................

his whole page to:
EEPOST CN81, Croydon, CR9 3WZ
0 Box 4546, Kilcock, County Kildare (stamp required)

UK and Eire only and not available to current Reader Service subscribers to this series. right to refuse an application and applicants must be aged 18 years or over. Only one ca er household. Terms and prices subject to change without notice. Dat January 2002. As a result of this application, you may receive offers from other Mill mpanies. If you would prefer not to share in this opportunity please write to The Medic address above.

gistered trademark owned by Harlequin Mills & Boon Limited. being used as a trademark.